MW01633941

SEARCHING FOR PANDORA (SPECIAL FORCES: OPERATION ALPHA)

FALLPORT RESCUE OPERATIONS
BOOK THREE

JEN TALTY

Dear Readers,

Welcome to the Special Forces: Operation Alpha Fan-Fiction world!

If you are new to this amazing world, in a nutshell the author wrote a story using one or more of my characters in it. Sometimes that character has a major role in the story, and other times they are only mentioned briefly. This is perfectly legal and allowable because they are going through Aces Press to publish the story.

This book is entirely the work of the author who wrote it. While I might have assisted with brainstorming and other ideas about which of my characters to use, I didn't have any part in the process or writing or editing the story.

I'm proud and excited that so many authors loved my characters enough that they wanted to write them into their own story. Thank you for supporting them, and me!

READ ON!
Xoxo
Susan Stoker

CHAPTER ONE

Blaze Wright rolled to a stop in front of Old Town Auto on Main Street in Fallport, Virginia. He put his shiny new pickup in park and let out a long breath. He'd been in the great state of Virginia before, but never Fallport, yet he felt as though he knew the place thanks to his old buddy, Brock Maybrey.

It had been four years since he'd seen Brock and a lot had happened.

Good things for Brock.

Not so good things for Blaze.

Blaze's life was shit. The majority of his problems were his own damn fault.

But some were not.

Either way, Blaze's life was going nowhere fast. His career in the Marines was over at forty. He'd given the military twenty-two years of his life and he honestly didn't regret a single day of it.

Except one.

And that day had been the reason he hadn't re-enlisted. Otherwise, he might have signed up for another four years. He wasn't that old. His body was in good shape. He could have done more time.

But he didn't have it in him. He had nothing left. His heart and soul were void. He'd spent the last four months figuring out if he could go on. The only answer he'd found was he didn't have the balls to put himself out of his misery. The only option left was to go west. He'd find a way to bury himself out there.

He had no one left and everything he owned was in the back of his new damn truck.

Pathetic when he thought about it, so he tried not to.

He shut off the engine and slipped from the vehicle. He'd made a promise to Brock and he'd be damned if he wasn't going to keep it. Although, part of him wanted to keep driving. Maybe to Colorado. Or Utah. He always loved hiking out there and there were many thrill-seeking opportunities that could get his adrenaline pumping and put his life in harm's way.

A memory of him and Brock hiking in Utah filled his brain. It had been one of the most exhilarating trips he'd ever been on. The best part about hiking with Brock was the man pushed Blaze, hard. And Brock didn't need to talk. Nope. He was one with nature.

It was refreshing to spend time with him and not have to discuss all of life's problems.

Only, this time, Blaze figured he wouldn't get away with keeping his shitty-ass life to himself because Brock had already hammered him once on the phone.

This would be a short trip. A day or two. Blaze couldn't stand to be where people knew him. Knew his past. Knew his pain.

Sucking in a deep breath, and mentally preparing himself for being a human, which was difficult these days, Blaze opened the door to his buddy's auto shop. A gentleman stood behind the counter.

"May I help you?" the man asked.

"Yeah. I'm here to see Brock. He's expecting me. The name's Blaze."

"Right. Brock's in the back. Go right ahead." The man pointed toward the door to the shop. "He's working on a blue vintage Mustang. You can't miss it."

"Thanks."

Blaze meandered through the shop, checking out all the cars. The Mustang was in the corner, but Brock wasn't with it.

The baby-blue vehicle was spectacular. It was a 1966 convertible and it was in mint condition. It looked damn fucking new and looked identical to the one he owned when he was twenty years old. He loved that damn fucking car.

Blaze ran his fingers across the side of the vehicle as he leaned inside to get a better look.

Damn, a stick. Just like he had and it was way too much fun to drive. He'd thought about buying a sports car when he'd left the military, but a truck made more sense, especially with the thought of being out west in the winter. The military had taught him to be practical, and regardless of the pull to have one of these bad boys, he couldn't pull the trigger.

"She's a beauty, isn't she?" an oddly familiar female voice said.

He froze, unable to turn his head toward the sound as his brain tried to reconcile that noise because no way in hell could it be *her*. He cleared his throat. "She sure is." He ran his fingers through his hair. It was longer than it had ever been since he'd been eighteen years old and he signed the enlistment papers. His parents had been so proud that day. Their son. A Marine. An honorable profession. Serving his country. Following in his big brother's footsteps.

And now Axel was dead and it was Blaze's fault.

He pushed that thought right out of his head and turned.

His heart plummeted to his toes like a rocket landing on its target and exploding with pure perfection.

"Jesus," Pandora whispered. "Blaze? Is that you?"

He rubbed the back of his neck, feeling the hair against his fingers as it tickled his skin. "Holy shit. Pandora. Un-fucking-believable."

"You can say that again." She inched closer as a slow smile spread across her angelic face. She was as beautiful as he remembered. Her hair was shorter, falling only to her shoulders instead of down to her waist, but he liked it that length. Her eyes were still as blue as the sea. Her hips were rounder and if he wasn't mistaken, her breasts might be bigger.

But now he was an asshole for staring at them.

He blinked.

"By the lack of a jarhead haircut, I'd say you're either on leave or out of the military." She leaned into him and gave him a brief hug and a kiss on the cheek.

"I just retired two months ago." He returned the favor, letting his lips linger on her sweet skin. She still smelled like coconut and roses. It was an intoxicating scent and he definitely didn't want to let his arms drop to his sides, but he did. He also stepped back, doing his best to regain some composure. "What the hell are you doing here?"

"I live here," she said.

He cocked a brow. "I have to say, that's shocking."

She laughed. "A lot has changed in twenty years." She leaned against the side of the Mustang. "What brings you to Fallport?"

"I'm here to see Brock. He's an old friend."

"Ah." She nodded. "He mentioned someone coming to visit; he just didn't give me a name."

"Where is he?" Blaze asked. Small talk wasn't his strong suit. Never was. And twenty years ago, Pandora used to tease him about his ability to sit in silence and not be bothered by it. But right now, silence would make him squirm, but he had no idea what to say.

Or how to act.

His heart still belonged to this woman, and his body knew it.

But his mind wasn't in the game. At all. And probably never would be.

Not after Axel.

"He's in the office. He had to make a phone call." She pointed to the Mustang. "This sweetheart is mine."

"You've got to be kidding me." He chuckled. "You finally learned to drive a stick." He shook his head. "I remember trying to teach you and I had the worst whiplash for days."

"I wasn't that bad." She gave him a little jab in the arm. "But the first car I bought on my own was a stick. You learn real quick when you no longer have a choice."

"That you do." He leaned against the hood and stuffed his hands in his jean pockets. "You look good."

"So do you," she said. "So, why did you leave the Marines?"

He ran his hand over his mouth. The only person, outside of the men in his unit, who knew the sordid details and his sister-in-law was Brock and he wasn't about to get into it with Pandora. Or anyone else for that matter. "It was time." He shrugged. "What have you been doing all these years?"

"I'm a firefighter and a paramedic."

"Really? I thought you were going to be a nurse."

"That's what my parents wanted me to do. But

again, a lot has changed." She jerked her head. "Here comes Brock."

Blaze pushed from the car. "Hey there, old man."

"Fuck off." Brock laughed, giving Blaze a big bro hug. "You're looking mighty scruffy. Welcome to civilian life."

"It's fucking weird, is what it is." Blaze smiled.

"I see you met Pandora and her car. I thought you might like it since you love a good vintage sports car," Brock said.

"Funny thing, Pandora and I actually knew each other a long time ago." Blaze still couldn't believe of all the people he could run into in this sleepy little town, it would be the girl he could never get out of his head. There had been many times he thought about looking for her, but then decided it wouldn't be right. She could be married with kids and he had no business messing with that.

"Well, I'll be damned." Brock slapped Blaze on the back. "Maybe she can show you around town since I'm slammed here and won't be free until at least six. Then you're coming to my place for dinner."

"I was about to go over to Sunny Side Up for some lunch," Pandora said. "You're welcome to join me, and then I'm happy to take a stroll through town and give you a little tour."

"I'd love that." Blaze nodded.

"All right. Hop in."

Blaze cocked his head. "I want to drive."

"Not happening, big fella." She jumped into the driver's seat. "Thanks for everything, Brock."

"Is my truck okay parked out front?" Blaze asked.

"Give me your keys. I'll have someone move it around back. Just in case your dumb ass parked it in a tow away zone." Brock laughed. "He's done that more times than I can count."

"He once got his Mustang towed in Myrtle Beach. It was a nightmare and he was pissed." Pandora laughed. "I guess some things don't change." She revved the engine. "Are you coming? Or are you too afraid to get in a car with me?"

"Utterly terrified." He tossed Brock his keys and slid into the passenger seat, buckling himself in. "How far away is this place?"

"Just around the corner. But maybe we can go for a little joyride first. I know a few back roads." She winked.

"Don't scare the boy." Brock knocked his knuckles on the hood. "And don't make Weston pull you over again. He's tired of not writing you tickets." Brock arched a brow. "Just because you're a first responder doesn't give you the right—"

"I got pulled over twice." She twisted her hair into a ponytail. "Once for failure to use my blinker and the other time I was doing ten over and Weston just likes to bust my balls." She released the emergency brake and put it in reverse. "Stop acting like my dad. I'll see you later and tell Finley thanks for the treats. The fire station always appreciates them."

"Drive safe." Brock waved.

"Why do I get the feeling this might be payback for taking you down that windy road in Lake George and scaring the crap out of you." Blaze gripped the holy shit bar as she turned the wheel, putting it in first gear.

"Because it is." She slowly eased out of the parking lot and onto the side street, then turned onto the main drag, passing his truck. They headed out of town and down a few more roads that he hadn't driven on his way to Fallport. Before he knew it, she was doing sixty on some curvy back street.

But to her credit, she handled the sports car like a pro.

And he wasn't scared shitless, like he honestly thought he would be.

She turned the car around and returned to town while playing music from the seventies. Something else that hadn't changed. They both loved to listen to that music. Classic rock. They would blast it from the radio while taking long drives and talking about nothing.

This was exactly like those days and he wasn't sure what to make of how it eased the ache in his soul. The pain in his heart.

Nothing could bring back his brother.

Blaze had gone over every step of that mission. His superiors had told him it didn't matter if he had made a different decision. The mission was doomed from the get-go. There had been a mole and his team had been compromised. Failure was the only option.

The mole had been caught and dealt with. He faced life in prison.

But again, that didn't change a damn thing.

And Blaze should have known there was a traitor in his ranks.

CHAPTER TWO

Pandora Maxwell spent the time in the car trying to figure out what the hell she'd say to Blaze at lunch. For years, she'd thought about what she'd tell him if she ever got the chance. She wrote letters that she never mailed. She'd collected her thoughts for almost two decades.

But now that she was face-to-face with the man who broke her heart—and whom she still loved—she had no words.

Nothing.

Nada.

Zilch.

Too much time had passed. There was nothing left to say.

Instead of going to straight to lunch, she opted to park and walk around town. She showed him where On The Rocks was so he could hang with all the guys from Search and Rescue. She showed him the places she thought he'd be interested in and chatted about the town, keeping the subject matter away from the past and firmly planted in the present.

And nothing personal.

But now it was time for lunch.

Blaze opened the door to the Sunny Side Up diner and they took a booth in the back. The diner wasn't too busy as most of the lunch crowd had already dwindled down.

"Where are you staying?" she asked, fiddling with her water glass, dunking the straw up and down, watching the ice cubes dance in the aqua.

"Red Caboose B and B." Blaze held the menu in his hands, as if to hide behind the laminated document.

Slowly, a band of awkward tension filled the space between them. There was no more coffee talk. No more inconsequential chatter left. It was just them and all the unspoken things they could never say to one another. Or at least she had never been brave enough to send those letters. She could have. He would have gotten them, at least those first few months after he sent his because she knew he was still stationed at Camp Lejeune for at least another half a year. But the death of her father and dealing with her mother had rocked her world in an unexpected way.

And he'd been right about one thing.

She did need to deal with her family, but not in the way he thought.

"That's not a bad place," she said. "How long are you in town for?"

"A few days, but Brock is trying to talk me into staying longer. He wants me to apply to the search and rescue team."

"They're a good group of men and women. It would be a good gig."

"I'm sure it would be. I just don't think it's right for me."

The waitress appeared at their table before she could ask or say anything else on that subject.

"Hey, Pandora," Janette said. "How ya doing today?"

"Great." Pandora nodded.

"Who's your friend?" Janette smiled.

"This is Blaze. He's a friend of Brock's and an old friend of mine." Why she decided to toss in that little piece of information, she wasn't sure, except Janette was always on the prowl for new meat. Every good-looking man not spoken for who came into town, Janette was all over. She was a nice girl but a bit desperate to get married and have babies. So much so that she had a reputation about it, making men run for the hills.

"Nice to meet you," Janette said. "If you need someone to show you around, I'm your girl."

Blaze chuckled. "Thanks. But I just got the million-dollar tour from Pandora."

"I see." Janette took out her little book and pencil. "Do you know what you want?"

"I'll have a double cheeseburger with a fried egg and onion rings. Can you also give me a side of potato salad? I know it's extra. And an iced tea." Pandora pushed her menu to the side.

"I see you still know how to pack in the food." Blaze chuckled. "Club sandwich, fries, and a Coke for me."

"Coming right up." Janette gathered the menus, tucking them under her arm, and jutted out her hip. "Maybe I'll see you over at On The Rocks sometime."

"I won't be here that long," Blaze said.

Janette turned and strolled away, swinging her hips.

Blaze had the nerve to lean out and look.

Pandora kicked him under the table.

"Ouch. What the hell did you do that for?"

"Staring at a woman's ass is rude." She cocked her head. "And if you're looking for a one-night stand, she's not the girl. She's looking to get a diamond and a baby. So unless you want to get trapped by her, I'd go look at someone else's ass if I were you."

"Well, you're sitting on yours, so I can't stare at it." He winked. "And for the record, I wasn't looking at her. I was checking out some dude giving me the stink eye and glaring at you."

She glanced over her shoulder. "Fuck," she mumbled, reaching in her bag and yanking out her cell. She found Weston's contact information.

Pandora: *I'm at Sunny Side Up and Sully's brother, Tim, is here with Carl.*

Weston: *On my way. Are you with anyone?*

"Who is that guy and who are you texting?" Blaze asked.

"Long story and I'm texting Weston."

Pandora: *Blaze Wright. He's a friend of Brock's and, oddly, an old friend of mine.*

"Is Weston your boyfriend or something?"

She burst out laughing. "God, no. He's a local cop and married to another local cop who happens to be a friend of mine." She blew out a puff of air, glancing over her shoulder again. Tim and Carl took seats at the counter. Their backs were to her, but that didn't make her feel any better about their presence. Sully got out tomorrow and he was pissed.

"So, who are those two over there, and why do they look like they want to hang us the old-fashioned way?"

"The guy with the man bun is Tim. His brother Sully is in prison. They blame me for Sully spending seven years there and Sully does too. He thinks he was wrongfully accused of attempted rape, which I was a witness to. For the last seven years, I've been dealing with their bullshit. I can't prove they've done anything, but the reason my car was in the shop was because some asshole took spray paint to it. I've had my house broken into and I've had threats made against me. But the kicker is that the day Sully got locked up, he made it clear he was coming for me, and he gets out tomorrow."

"Well, shit." Blaze shifted in his seat, resting his arm

over the back of the booth. "Has this guy Sully made threats since he's been in prison?"

"Nope. But he still claims he's innocent. That he and this girl were role-playing a rape."

Blaze arched a brow. "While I'm not into that shit, I'm sure some people have done it."

"Sure they have. But that's not what this was and the girl in question testified to that, but Sully believes I put all that shit in her head. His attorney came at me on the stands with both guns blazing. They tried to tear me down. They found every blemish on my record. Every little thing about my past and did their best to discredit me, and it nearly worked, but Andrea's testimony put the asshole behind bars."

"Not that it's any of my business, but how did they discredit you?"

"It doesn't matter."

"Maybe not, but if this guy Sully wants revenge, you might not see it coming. It might not be in the form of violence." Blaze arched a brow. "So, what did they use on the stand that made you look bad?"

She might not know Blaze anymore, but she knew his character, the kind of man he was. And she knew without a doubt that this would be more than painful for him to hear.

Even more painful for her to tell.

A single tear rolled down her cheek. She could tell him about the few screwups at work that the attorney used to make her look incompetent and reckless. Or how they used her failed marriage to try to paint her as a bitter woman toward men.

However, none of those things were strong enough, and the real issue of her testimony had become ineffective for the DA. It had been a calculated risk putting her on the stand, but she was the only witness.

Blaze reached across the table and wiped her tear away. "Come on, Pandora, talk to me."

"You have to promise me you won't get up and do anything stupid."

He lowered his chin.

"Eight years ago, I was working a fire. It wasn't a bad one. We didn't know it at the time, but the damn fire was set on purpose. I was one of the first to enter the building. I got caught in the back room after a beam came down. There was a window, but it was small. I had to take off some of my gear to get out. Someone was outside and helped pull me through that fucking window. I never saw who it was. They wore a ski mask."

"Jesus Christ." Blaze's hand came down hard on the table. The water glasses sloshed. "Were they waiting for you?"

"We don't know. My captain could never tell if that beam came down because of the fire or if it was on purpose."

"What did that man do to you?" Blaze asked with a growl in his tone, holding her gaze with rage-filled eyes.

She turned, unable to look at him a second longer. "He dragged me into the woods. Tied me up. Beat the crap out of me. Broke a few ribs. Punctured a lung. Cracked my cheekbone. My eyes were so swollen for days I couldn't even open them," she said softly.

"Did he rape you?"

She sucked in a breath, but no air filled her lungs. She nodded.

"And they never caught the guy, right? That's why Sully's attorney was able to rip you up on the stands. He made you out to be an angry victim, unable to handle the role-play, and he victimized you on the stands all over again."

She snapped her gaze back to Blaze's. "He might have laid into me and used that against my testimony, but I held my own. I didn't allow him to push me into being a victim."

"But your rape is still an open case and that attorney used it to make it seem like you wanted revenge on any man."

"Something like that," she whispered.

"Are there any leads? DNA? Anything?" Blaze asked.

"This is where it gets real fun," she said. "My fellow firefighters had come looking for me and found him cleaning me up. One of them, Greg, chased him through the woods, but never caught him, while everyone else tended to me. But that house was owned by Sully and his brother, Tim."

"That can't be a fucking coincidence."

"There's no proof. There was no semen. I didn't get the chance to scratch him and get his skin under my nails. I couldn't even fight because he clocked me with a rock as soon as he pulled me out that window. I was dazed and confused. To be honest, I barely remember what happened. Only the aftermath. The worst part is both Tim and Sully have rock-solid alibis and during Andrea's trial, I was made out to be a woman who was after them."

"And now he's coming for you." Blaze reached across the table and took her hands. "Do you have a husband? A boyfriend? Someone living with you?"

"Nope."

"What do the cops plan on doing once Sully is released?"

"He'll be on probation and will have to answer to that department. Weston, my friend, has promised he'll increase patrols around my home. I sleep at the station when I'm working, but what else can they do?"

"Sometimes our justice system sucks."

Janette approached, carrying their food and drinks on a tray. She placed their order on the table and smiled. "Can I get you folks anything else?" She set a piece of paper in front of Blaze.

"We're good," Blaze said. "Thanks."

Janette frowned when Blaze didn't even look at what she left him. She turned on her heel and strolled away.

He lifted the paper and crumpled it up.

"What was that?"

"Her number and I'm not interested." He dunked it in his water and pulled out his cell.

"What are you doing?"

"Canceling my reservation at the Red Caboose B and B. Consider me your personal bodyguard for the foreseeable future."

"Blaze. First, my apartment is tiny. It's a one-bedroom."

"I'll sleep on the sofa." He continued tapping on the screen of his phone. "Next."

"You're here on vacation and to visit with Brock."

"It's my vacation to spend how I see fit and Brock has a life. A wife. He's busy and I'll need things to fill my time. Any other objections?" he asked.

"Yeah. I don't want you living with me."

"I won't be. I'm just a guest until we find a way to nail that asshole and send him back where he belongs." He set his cell face down on the table. "Tell me some-thing. How did you spend the year from when you were raped and the time Sully went to prison? Did you leave your house? Did you feel safe? Could you go places and not look over your shoulder? Or were you ruled by fear because that asshole got away with it?"

"That's not fair. Of course I was terrified. It was fresh. It was the single most horrifying experience of my life. You can't even imagine what I went through."

"No, I can't and honestly, my brain is struggling with the entire concept. Men can be such assholes and no woman—no human—deserves that. But you also shouldn't have to live in fear. At least I can help a little bit with that, I hope."

She leaned back, dropped her head to the booth, and stared at the ceiling. A few people had offered for her to come and stay with them. Friends from the station. Weston and Haven. A few of the guys from Search and Rescue. Even Brock. But they all had lives. Families. Children. And she couldn't live with them forever.

And she sure as shit wasn't going to run from a town that had become her home.

But she knew deep in her soul that Sully had raped her. She couldn't prove it. She hadn't seen his face. Barely got a glimpse of his eyes. But her heart and mind knew it had been him. And he'd sat in that court-room, smiling at her with that same knowledge, knowing he'd gotten away with it.

"Let me help you, Pandora. I've got nothing to do and nowhere to go." Blaze lifted his sandwich and took a bite.

"What about your family?"

He dropped his food, which landed with a thud on his plate. "They're gone. My folks died in a plane crash five years ago and Axel died four months ago."

"Oh, Blaze. I'm so sorry. I didn't know."

"You couldn't have." He tapped his finger on her burger. "Eat your food, and then we'll leave. You'll drive me to my truck and I'll follow you home. I'll tell

Brock we'll have to do dinner on a night you're working at the firehouse."

"I don't want you to—"

"No arguments. It's settled."

"You're still so bossy." She sliced her burger into halves and bit into the greasy delight, doing her best to ignore the dangers that lurked in the background.

"How are your parents?"

"My father died twenty years ago. Actually, a couple of months after we broke up. And my mom?" She shook her head, laughing. "She remarried some hippie and is smoking pot and macrodosing mushrooms. She's a total wacko and lives in California these days. Although, they move like every two years."

Blaze stared at her with his mouth gaping open.

"I know. It's not what you would have expected from the woman who might have well put me in a chastity belt."

"Damn. I only met your mother once and she broke out in prayer. I was waiting for her to start speaking in tongues or try an exorcism on me or something."

"She did believe you were the devil."

Blaze chuckled. "I was a good little boy. You were the one who was the bad influence. You talked me into going to that underground bar. I so thought we were going to die that night."

She rolled her eyes. "It wasn't that bad and you did win fifty dollars in pool."

"We did have some good times together." He raised

his Coke and took a gulp. "Now finish up so we can get out of here before flirty pants comes back and makes me do something crazy."

"You'd actually go out with her?"

"God, no. But if she tries to give me her number again, I might have to slide over there and give you an inappropriate kiss that will drive a specific point home."

"You wouldn't dare."

"Wanna bet? Because here she comes." He stood and slipped in beside her, resting his hand on her thigh. He leaned in close, his lips touching her cheek. "I'll do it," he whispered.

"Is everything to your liking?" Janette asked with a scrunched-up face as if she'd swallowed a lemon.

It was funny and made Pandora smile. Lord knew she needed some lightness in her life right about now.

"Food's good. Company's even better." Blaze squeezed her leg as he gazed into her eyes, ignoring Janette.

"Can I get you anything else?" Janette asked.

"Just the check and a couple of boxes. I think we'll take the rest home with us, right, babe?" He traced her jawline with his index finger.

She held her breath as he pressed his mouth firmly against her lips, slipping his tongue between them in an all too familiar tango. It was short, but it packed a powerful reminder of the heat they once shared.

"Um, yeah. Sure. No problem," Janette said, disappearing between the tables.

"That was mean," Pandora said softly.

"But it killed two birds with one stone."

"What does that mean?"

"It got her off my back," Blaze said. "And let those two idiots know you're not alone. They will tell Sully about me and he will think twice about coming anywhere near you."

"And what happens when you leave in a few days?" That was a question she shouldn't have asked.

"Like I said, I have nothing going on and nowhere to be."

And with that, her world flipped into a tailspin and she wasn't sure what to make of anything. But for now, she'd take his help because he was right. Once Sully was released and back in Fallport, fear would become a way of life again and that was no way to live.

CHAPTER THREE

Blaze stared at the sofa bed in Pandora's apartment in town. It was a nice little place in a four-story building, but it was tiny as fuck. And he hated that she was on the first floor. That was a security nightmare.

But he'd deal with it.

"I have no idea if that thing is comfortable or not." She appeared from the bedroom that was behind the small eat-in kitchen, holding a set of sheets. "I've never even opened it before. When Weston and Haven moved into their house, they gave it to me. Weston said he never opened it but slept on it and mentioned it wasn't horrible. It's comfy to watch TV on."

"I'll manage. I've slept in some pretty shitty places during my time in the military." He pointed toward the door. "I like your locks. I'm glad you aren't fucking around with safety."

"Weston and Greg installed them after the rape."

"Who's Greg?"

"My ex-husband." She pursed her lips.

"Not sure why I'm asking this, but before or after the rape?"

"After." She set the sheets on the small chair next to the fireplace and found the fitted one.

He took one end and helped her tug it over the mattress.

"He's the one who went after my attacker. He sat with me every night at the hospital. He was there when I woke up after being in a medically induced coma for two weeks because of the concussion and swelling in my brain. I had no idea he cared that much until that happened to me. We got married two years later. It barely lasted that long."

"Because of what happened?"

She shook her head as she placed the other sheet on top and then tossed him a pillow and a case for it. "While I loved him, or maybe the idea of him, it wasn't enough for a marriage. I never fully committed, but it had nothing to do with the rape." She opened a drawer from the coffee table and handed him a blanket. "It gets pretty warm in here at night. I can turn up the AC if you want me to."

"I'm sure I'll be fine."

"There's also a fan in that closet."

"Did you and your husband live here?" Jesus, what the fuck was wrong with him? One kiss and he thought he had the right to know her life story?

"No. He owned a home so I moved in there. A friend of Haven's moved in here, but she fell for some FBI guy and moved away, which was nice because I like this building. And this apartment."

"I don't like it being on the first floor." He pointed toward the windows. "Easy access for predators. If you don't mind, I want access to your security cameras."

"You can download the app and I can get you the passwords. Weston has access too. I'll introduce you to him tomorrow. He's a good man."

"You said his wife's a cop too?" Blaze spread out the blanket and then flopped onto the bed. His ass hit a metal rung.

Wonderful.

He stretched out his legs, crossing his ankles, and stared at Pandora, who sat on the fireplace hearth.

"She is and a good one too." Pandora fiddled with her fingernails, something she did when she was nervous.

He couldn't blame her for that. He just hoped he wasn't adding to it.

"I'm so sorry to hear about your brother. I know how close the two of you were."

Well, shit. That was a conversation he didn't want to have.

"Thank you," he said.

"What happened?"

"I really don't want to talk about it and honestly, I

can't," he said. "He died on a mission and you know there are things in the military I just can't discuss."

She closed her eyes and nodded as if she understood. But she didn't. No one did. She blinked. "So, what about you? Ever been married? Kids? Any of that?"

Leave it to her to switch gears to something else he didn't want to shoot the shit about. But what the hell. She'd told him a shit ton in just a few short hours, so he could suffer through his shitty relationship. "I'll need a beer—or better yet some of that tequila I saw in the kitchen—before telling that sob story."

"Coming right up." She jumped to her feet and rustled up a couple of glasses and brought the bottle. She poured two tumblers and handed him one before making herself comfortable in his bed. Next to him.

How dare her.

Well, shit.

He sipped his drink and contemplated where to start.

"How long were you married? Or is that still a thing?" she asked.

"Newly divorced. Though we were separated for two years before getting around to making it official."

"How long were you married?"

"Technically, we would have celebrated ten years right before we signed the papers, but the last five years we might as well have been done." He took another sip and let the alcohol fill his brain.

"Come on, Blaze. I can sit here and keep asking questions, or you can just talk."

"I hate talking about feelings and real shit and you know it." He chuckled. "But if you must know, Ashley, my ex-wife, always believed that the past lived in our marriage. That I was never fully present, and honestly, she was right. I asked her to marry me because it's what I thought I was supposed to do. I was pushing thirty and most men in my unit were getting married and having babies. I'd been with Ashley for almost two years, and she had hinted that marriage and family were next."

"Did you feel trapped?"

He shook his head. "It wasn't that. And for the record, I did love my wife, but like you, it wasn't *set your world on fire* love. It was the idea of it all. Someone to come home to after being deployed. Someone's picture to hold while on the back of some plane going to some danger zone, wondering if you're going to come back alive."

"For over a year, that picture used to be me," she whispered.

He let out a long breath. "And that right there was one of the biggest problems."

"What does that mean?" She jerked her head.

Well, fuck. He'd gone and done it now. That was just plain fucking stupid. And he couldn't even chalk it up to too much tequila. He tossed the rest of his drink back in one gulp and reached for the bottle, filled his glass, and did it again. He'd come this far in his confession, so he might as well go for broke. What difference did it make?

They were different people. In a different place. There were twenty years between now and when they'd planned a future together until her parents put an end to it.

And he'd let them.

It was over.

One kiss meant nothing.

Time to purge this part of his life.

He pulled his wallet out of his back pocket and rifled through the contents until he found the faded, worn image that had gotten him through some of his worst nightmares. He ran his fingers over the torn edges before handing it to her. "Ashley found this about five years into our marriage. Mind you, we already had problems. And big ones. This was just the nail in the coffin."

"Jesus. You still have this thing?" She glanced between her senior picture and him with wide eyes. "I don't know if I'm flattered or mortified."

"You should be a little of both." He snagged the picture and tucked it back in his billfold before setting it on the end table.

"I would have kicked your sorry ass out of the house."

"Well, I was leaving for two months and thought I

might not have a home to return to, but we went to counseling when I did get back."

"I don't even want to think about what might have been said."

He burst out laughing.

"I don't find that funny at all."

"It's kind of hilarious because we didn't spend all that much time talking about you."

"Now I'm insulted."

"Don't be. Like I said, our marital problems weren't really about you."

"Um, you were carrying around a picture of your ex-girlfriend. That's enough to make any wife lose her shit."

"True, but my inability to let go of that picture was only one reason I had a foot out the door before we even got married. The truth is I should have never proposed in the first place. Whether I loved her or not, it wasn't enough. I loved my career more."

"She wanted you to give it up?"

"Yes and no. She wanted me to do what some of my friends had done and take a different post. Something where I wouldn't be deployed all the time and would be at one base for years. Instead, I volunteered for my brother's division, which meant more dangerous missions. It meant I was gone more, and Ashley hated that. Resented me for doing it and I was an asshole because of it."

"If you didn't discuss it with her, yeah, that was a

dick move." She covered his mouth. "But she knew who you were when she married you. She didn't have the right to try to change you. However, the picture? That's a different story."

"Marines can be superstitious and I took that picture on my first deployment and that was a shit show. Two men died."

She turned, palming his cheek. "I remember. You were a mess. You took a week leave and came to my dorm."

"I would have never made it through that without you." He kissed her hand. "I hid that picture from Ashley after she found it the first time. It had less to do with you or her and more to do with that first mission. I tried to tell her that, but she didn't understand."

"While I get a little bit about what you went through, I'm not sure I understand that, but I won't take away your feelings about it and I'm glad an image could help you through some dark times."

A bit of guilt tugged at his heart. "To be fair, part of it was you, but I couldn't see that. Not right away." He took another sip of his beverage. "I don't know. It was so long ago and most people move past their first loves. Ours was riddled with secret rendezvous. We were never able to bask in how we felt. You had some shame in that and it always tore me up that you were forced to choose." He released her hand. "But that was a lifetime ago and once Ashley and I divorced, a few things became clear."

"Like what?"

"Letting go of her allowed me to let go of old ideals. I wasn't cut out to be a husband. A father. A family man. My life was fulfilled in the Marines. When I was deployed, I was happy. When I was home, I was miserable."

"Then why did you leave?"

"Axel," he whispered before downing the rest of his drink. "It's late. We should get some sleep." He would not go down that dark and slippery road. If he did, he might pack his bags and leave in the middle of the night.

And he couldn't do that to her.

Not when she needed someone to protect her.

He'd deal with his emotions about his brother another time.

Only, he didn't know how to do that.

CHAPTER FOUR

After a long night of tossing and turning on the worst bed known to man, Blaze pulled his T-shirt over his head and padded to the kitchen to scrounge up a cup of coffee.

It wasn't just the metal bars digging into his back that had caused a rough night. It was the woman sleeping two rooms away. For twenty years, she'd always been in the back of his mind, creeping into his thoughts when he'd least expect it, even though he'd accepted that part of his life was over. The picture in his wallet might have weaved a different story, but he'd been telling the truth about how there had been some superstition to his reason behind keeping it. He had a ritual before every mission and it hadn't changed. While he knew in his heart of hearts it wasn't the ritual that had kept him alive, or the image, he still had to do it.

The marriage counselor that he and Ashley went to actually understood that, but the therapist had been a military man who saw action. And he spoke to many men like Blaze who watched their brothers-in-arms die on the battlefield. However, no amount of discussing how Blaze believed that single image had brought him out of that mission alive, where half the men on his team had come home in body bags, was going to make Ashley believe keeping the picture was a healthy thing. In the end, the therapist wondered if Blaze could slowly find a new ritual.

So, Blaze lied and said he'd work on it.

Six months later he had his wife believing he was using a picture of his parents. The problem with that was it wasn't a photograph of Ashley.

He found a mug and one of those pod things. He placed it in the machine and hit the start button. He could hear Pandora moving about in her room. He checked the time. Only eight in the morning.

Ding-dong.

He glanced over his shoulder, but the door to her bedroom didn't open. He sighed and made his way through the small apartment and snagged his weapon. He peered through the peephole and stared at a man he didn't know. It wasn't Tim or Carl. And it wasn't Sully because he'd gotten a picture of what that asshole looked like.

With his weapon at his side, he unlocked the door and opened it.

The man looked him up and down. "You're Blaze." He held up his hands. "That gun isn't necessary."

"You know who I am, but I'm at a disadvantage, because I don't have a clue as to who you are."

"I'm Greg."

"Ah. The ex-husband." Blaze waved Greg in, setting his weapon on the end table. "Sorry for the aggressive way I answered the door."

"No worries. I'm just glad she's not alone, but I didn't expect to see you here, much less ever meet you."

Blaze wasn't sure what to make of this encounter. The only thing he knew of this man was that he had loved Pandora enough to marry her, but that it hadn't lasted. However, Blaze didn't really understand why. What she'd told him didn't add up any more than his original story about the breakup of his marriage. There was more to that story, but he'd said enough. He'd shown Pandora the picture that he'd never let go of.

She'd been a ghost in his marriage whether he wanted to admit it or not.

"Jesus, that thing couldn't have been comfortable to sleep on." Greg pointed to the pullout.

"It was the pits." Blaze laughed. "Do you want some coffee?"

"I'd love some," Greg said. "Where's Pandora?"

"I haven't seen her yet this morning, but I think she's in the shower." Blaze lifted the freshly brewed coffee from the machine and handed it to Greg. "I assume the creamer's in the fridge, but no idea where the sugar is."

"I take it black."

"Me too." He found another mug, tossed out the old pod, and put in a new one. He tapped the button and leaned against the counter. "So, what brings you by this early?"

"A few things, but mostly, I didn't want her to be alone today. I have no idea what you know about what's going on—"

"I know enough." Blaze folded his arms across his chest. "And I don't plan on letting her out of my sight."

Just then, the bedroom door flung open and in strolled Pandora. She wore a pair of jean shorts, a black tank top, and her wet hair dipped just past her shoulders. "Greg, why on earth are you here?"

Greg pulled a folded piece of paper from his back pocket. "I brought you a revised schedule for the fire station. I made sure that our schedules match. I figured if we worked the same shifts, you'd never have to be alone."

She squeezed Greg's biceps.

A gesture that for some reason annoyed the fuck out of Blaze and it shouldn't. That was her ex-husband. They had a bond. One that had nothing to do with him.

"First, our captain emailed those changes this morning and copied the entire crew, including you." She lowered her chin. "Second, shouldn't you be doing wedding planning shit with Bonnie?"

Greg rolled his eyes. "This is a second marriage for both of us. No idea why we have to have a wedding. It's ridiculous."

"Because you both eloped the first time." She lifted the mug of coffee from the machine and sipped.

Blaze groaned, pulling down a third mug as he went through the whole coffee making process. Again.

"Besides, Bonnie doesn't want some big extravagant thing. Just a simple wedding. In a church. With her family and friends. I don't think it's too much to ask." Pandora leaned against the sink.

"Great. My ex-wife is taking my future wife's side. Wonderful." Greg waggled his finger between Pandora and Blaze. "So, how did the two of you get in touch after all these years?"

"I feel like I should take an ad in the paper," Pandora said. "Blaze happens to be friends with Brock. We ran into each other yesterday. Totally out of the blue. I took him to lunch, where we ran into Tim and Carl, and I ended up telling him about Sully, so Blaze, in true *Blaze of Glory* fashion, took it upon himself to be my bodyguard."

"Good. I'm glad, especially when you refuse to listen to reason and stay with someone." Greg arched a brow. "Bonnie and I would have had no problem with you moving in for a while and we have plenty of room."

"Right. Me shacking up with my ex and his future bride wouldn't have been awkward," she mumbled.

"Is it awkward having an ex on your pullout?" Greg arched a brow.

"Yes," she said.

"I'm offended." Blaze took the fresh mug and brought it to his lips. Damn, that was good. Lord knew he needed the caffeine.

"Well, since you really don't need me and Bonnie does want me to go taste cakes and other treats with Finley this morning, I'll be on my way." He rinsed his mug out in the sink. "But, Pandora, please don't hesitate to call if you need anything at all." He took her by the shoulders. "I will always care about you and I was there when that… when… just call me." He kissed her cheek. "You should give Blaze my number in case he can't be by your side, or if he needs backup for any reason."

"Thanks, Greg," Pandora said. "Say hello to Bonnie."

"Will do." Greg stretched out his arm. "It was nice to meet you."

"You as well." Blaze stayed in the kitchen while Pandora walked her ex-husband to the door. A few faint words were exchanged, but Blaze couldn't hear them.

She shuffled back into the kitchen.

"Greg seems like a stand-up guy." Blaze blew into his coffee and took a healthy swig.

"He's a good man. The best. I hurt him and I feel bad about that. I'm just glad we've managed to be friends and that he's found someone who makes him happy, because he would have never been if he stayed with me."

Blaze threaded his fingers through his hair, contemplating his next words. "I know you said your divorce wasn't because of the rape. But I'm left wondering what really happened between the two of you because it's obvious he still cares about you and I certainly wouldn't kick him out of bed."

That last little bit put a smile on her face.

Blaze was grateful his odd sense of humor could do that.

"If you're asking if what happened to me affected me and my ability to let a man touch me, of course it did. But like I said, Greg is a good man. A patient, kind, and loving one. He was there for me. He even went to the therapist with me. I swear he would have waited years for me to be ready and that's probably why I fell in love with him, but that's not enough to sustain a marriage. A friendship, sure. But it's not what builds a life together."

"So, what you're telling me is there was no spark. No passion."

"Why do you want to know so badly?" She slammed her mug on the counter and glared, as if he'd just asked the worst question in the world.

"I spent ten years with a woman, and while I wanted to love her because she did have some amazing qualities and she made me laugh, she didn't understand me. She didn't get what drove me and certainly didn't try to comprehend it. You had someone who got you and went above and beyond to make sure all your needs were met. I'm trying to understand why that would fail."

"Do you really want the truth?"

"Of course I do."

"After you and I broke up, I was a bit of a hot mess. But after my father died just a few short months later, my entire world went upside down."

He inched closer and curled his fingers around her forearm.

"This isn't easy for me to tell." She shrugged it away and turned, walking toward the family room. She climbed up onto the pullout and hugged one of the pillows.

He opted for the small chair next to the sofa bed. "I'm listening."

She fiddled with her wet hair and sighed. "My mother was lost without my dad. He controlled every-thing. He ruled our house with an iron fist. Whatever he said was what was expected. I had always believed my parents were on the same page because my mother was often just as bad as he was and in some ways worse. She was the one who took me clothes shopping and never let me buy what I wanted. Nothing too revealing. No bikinis."

He chuckled. "You had some tiny ones when we met."

"That's because I bought them when I got to Myrtle Beach, along with all these skimpy outfits. I could be free for those two weeks. The fact that they even let me go was a fucking miracle."

"You were an adult."

"I was still in high school. I had just turned eighteen. But one of my friends' parents lied to my folks, saying we were staying with their family, not in some musty old run-down hotel off the strip. They believed we were being chaperoned the entire time. I got in so much trouble when I got home and they learned otherwise," she said.

"I'm not sure I understand how this has anything to do with your divorce."

"I'm getting there, if you'd stop interrupting me." She glared.

He raised his hands, showing his palms. If she needed a trip down memory lane, he'd give it to her.

"My mother didn't know what to do with herself after my dad died. She had no clue about their finances, or even where their money was. I had to help her go through all the stuff in my dad's office. During those next few months, my mom would constantly break down and cry. She started opening up to me about how utterly abusive my father had been."

"Physically?"

Pandora nodded. "I never saw him hit her. He never put a bruise on her face, but she said he'd punch her in the gut when she'd ask him to lighten up with me. When she'd privately go to bat for me." She swiped a tear from her cheek. "I had no idea. I also didn't know that my parents got married because my mom had been pregnant with me. That she hadn't necessarily wanted the marriage, or me."

"Jesus, that's a tough pill to swallow."

"Tell me about it," she said. "Once my mother shared that, things really changed. She told me it was time for her to take back her life, and that's exactly what she did, without me in it. She apologized to me, as if that would make her selfishness for needing to be her own woman sting less. She sold the house, got an apartment in the heart of town, and started dating. A lot. She was a completely different person. She told me this was who she'd been when she met my father. She told me that when they first got married, he wasn't this crazy man who expected her to be the good little wife, but slowly, he took away all her power, and she found herself trapped. Her life no longer her own. Anyway, now that she was single, and I was an adult, she felt as though she could finally have the life she deserved. I'm now merely an afterthought."

"I'm sure your mother loves you," Blaze said.

"I'm not saying she doesn't. But she cares more about her current husband and their life than she does me." Pandora hugged the pillow tighter. "When I was raped, I called her to tell her what happened. All I wanted was my mom. She was at some weird hippie retreat and couldn't get away for three weeks. She told me she'd come after that."

Blaze closed his eyes and counted to ten. He couldn't imagine that. His parents were at his side every single time he needed them, and sometimes when he hadn't wanted them, until the day they died. God, how he missed them. "What happened when she came to visit?"

"She didn't." Pandora chuckled. "She called when the retreat ended and asked if I still needed her because there was a road trip she was invited on and it was going to be epic. I told her to go. That I'd be fine."

"I'm sorry." He had no other words.

"She showed up four months later. She pampered me for three days. It was nice, but it was a little too late."

"I'd say so."

"Greg was so wonderful during that time. His love was unconditional and it was the first time I had felt that since—well, you. It was intoxicating. It was all-consuming. I couldn't get enough of it. I wanted to drown in it. I gobbled it up like it was the best frosting on a birthday cake. Oddly, it also reminded me of when I was a kid. It was safe. Secure. It wasn't like Greg was anything like my parents because he wasn't. But Greg likes structure. We call him the color-coding king at the fire station because he is so fucking organized. But after our first anniversary, it started to feel like I had a noose around my neck." She laughed, shaking her head. "He has this label machine and used it to make little labels for all the switches in the house so you know which switch controls which light. I mean, the house was big and it made sense. But it drove me bonkers and I wanted to rip those fuckers off the wall because it started to remind me of how controlling my father was, but again, Greg's nothing like that man. I was just starting to realize I married him for all the wrong reasons."

"You married him because he loved you the way you needed to be loved, only your love for him was because of that. Not because you loved the man," Blaze said, rubbing his temples. Why he felt responsible for her failed marriage was beyond him. It wasn't his fault. Honestly, it was no one's fault except hers and Greg's. And they came through it much easier than most divorced couples.

And he knew that from experience.

"I'm sorry I wasn't there for you when your father died. I didn't know."

"You made it clear we were done. I didn't feel as though it was my place to burden you with that."

He stood and eased onto the uncomfortable mattress. He looped his arm around her shoulders. "I want you to know that a part of me will always regret not fighting for us." He kissed her temple. "For months I thought about reaching out. I wrote you letters, begging for forgiveness, but then I'd toss them into the trash, not wanting to force you to choose between your family and me."

"Because your family means the world to you."

"They sure did." His chest tightened. He'd failed his parents the day his brother died in his arms. But he couldn't think about that right now. He'd deal with that after he helped Pandora. He could get her through this time until Sully was behind bars. Then he'd drown himself in some good tequila until the day came when he too would meet his maker.

He didn't have a death wish. It wasn't about physically dying anymore. But it sure as shit wasn't about living because that died with Axel, and his brother's widow and two children needed Axel more than they needed Blaze. But Blaze couldn't bring his brother back.

"I was hurt when you didn't show up the day we were planning on running away to get married. My parents and Axel were excited for us. I had more than a bruised ego. But I did try to put myself in your shoes. I didn't want to put pressure on you and thought if I cut you loose, it would be for the best. I want to believe that was the right decision, for both of us. We can't go back and change the past, but since we're talking about it again, I feel the need to share that sometimes I wonder if letting you go the way I did wasn't a coward move."

She laughed. "We were both so young. You were

twenty. I was nineteen. What the hell did we know. Besides, I can honestly say that outside of a few traumatic experiences, I've loved my life here in Fallport and I bet you can say the same for your life in the Marines."

"I can," he said.

"And since we're being honest, I don't know if I would have had the bandwidth to deal with you and my mother after my dad died. Trust me when I say that first year was hell."

"Fair enough.

She reached out and palmed his cheek. "What happened to Axel?"

Every muscle in his body stiffened. He slipped from the bed. "I'm not ever going to speak of that, so please don't ask me again." He made a beeline for the kitchen and another cup of joe. He stood in front of the machine and tapped his fingers on the counter.

A warm hand touched the back of his neck.

"Talking about it might do you a world of good," she whispered as her lips pressed against his shoulder.

A deep growl filled his throat. It took every ounce of resolve he had not to push her away. He didn't want to hurt her, but if he was going to be able to stay, he had to make this clear. "Don't."

"Blaze—"

"I said stop it." He shrugged her off and turned to face her. "This is one topic that isn't up for discussion and I'd appreciate it if you never brought up his name again. I need to go get cleaned up. When I'm done, we can go out for breakfast, or I'll cook. Whatever you like." He stormed off toward her bedroom, toward the only shower in the house, leaving his coffee under the machine. He'd drink it later, after he cooled off.

CHAPTER FIVE

Pandora couldn't leave well enough alone. She flipped open her laptop and googled Axel Wright.

She found his wife's social media profiles, most of which were set to private, though a few images were available. They had two little boys who looked just like their dad and uncle. So cute.

Then she found the obituary.

It gave the date of his death and the time and place of the services at the very beginning. And then it went into a short paragraph about his life.

Axel Wright joined the Marines at the age eighteen and served until he was killed in the line of duty. He died a true hero. He was awarded the Purple Heart. He is survived by his wife, Brenda, and two boys, Blaze and Marvin, named after his brother and father. He's also survived by his brother, Blaze Wright, a fellow Marine, who was awarded the Combat Action Ribbon and the Marine Corps Expedi-

tionary Medal for his service. Axel was a brother to all who knew him and he will be missed.

One thing Pandora knew for sure was that Blaze did not write that obituary. He would never want his medals displayed for public consumption. It must have been Brenda.

The water turned off and Pandora quickly closed out her search and closed the computer, no closer to finding out what happened to Axel or why Blaze wouldn't talk about it. Other than maybe it was too fresh. That she could understand.

Blaze and Axel had been best friends growing up. They were only eighteen months apart. They did everything together and she'd met Axel a dozen times. He and Blaze were so much alike, and yet so different. They had all the same mannerisms and looked nearly identical, though Blaze had two inches on his big brother and Axel had a scar on his chin. Blaze's sense of humor was a little dryer, but Axel was a prankster, always pulling dumb jokes on his little brother.

Their dream had always been to be in the same unit in the Marines. To work side by side.

She dropped her head to the table as a horrible thought filled her brain.

If Axel and Blaze had managed to be on the same unit and Axel died during a mission they were both on, and Blaze didn't, that would fuck with any man.

Blaze stepped from her bedroom, wearing only a towel. "Sorry. I left my clothes out there." He pointed toward the family room with a handful of wadded-up clothes. "I'm going to have to do laundry soon. I didn't notice a washer or dryer anywhere, so you're going to have to tell me where the nearest laundromat is."

"In that closet over there. But it's a tiny machine, so be careful how much you put in it."

"No worries." He strolled past her in his towel. "Stay in here. I'm going to change in the family room."

Her gaze followed him into the other room. She leaned across the table, unable to take her eyes off a fine specimen of a man. He was a little thicker in the middle than he used to be, but wasn't everyone twenty years later? He still had a six-pack, though. But it was the scars on his body that gave her pause. There were a lot of them and some of them were fresh. She could tell as they were pink around the edges and still raised. She wanted to trace her fingers over them and ask about each and every single one.

Some were long and jagged.

Others looked as though they could be from a bullet.

A few looked like burn marks.

The things he must have seen in the military nearly broke her heart.

He dropped his towel and she let out an audible groan as she stared at his taut ass.

"Are you taking in a peep show?" He hiked up his boxers and turned.

She hadn't moved, nor had her gaze. "Sorry. I

couldn't help myself. Besides you still being incredibly sexy, I couldn't help but notice all the scars," she admitted.

"Shit happens. Not a big deal." He stepped into his jeans and yanked up his zipper. When she'd met him, she'd been a virgin. But he certainly wasn't and he also hadn't been shy about his body. He walked around naked all the time. At first, it embarrassed the hell out of her, but as she fell in love with him and became comfortable in her own skin, being naked with him was as natural as apple pie.

He meandered into the kitchen and snagged the mug under the coffee machine, still shirtless. As if to taunt her with his muscular body.

She waved her finger at his chest. "Those look like kind of a big deal."

"Not worth having a discussion over." Glancing down, he ran his free hand over his stomach. "What would you like to do about breakfast? Because I'm starving."

Before she could answer, her phone buzzed. She picked it up from the table and glanced at the screen. "Fuck."

"What is it?"

"A text from Weston," she mumbled. "Sully is two hours away from rolling into town."

Blaze took a swig from his coffee, set the mug on the counter, and closed the gap. He rested his hand on her shoulder. "The man would be a fool to come after you the second he came back."

"Maybe so, but you weren't there the day the jury came back with the guilty verdict. Or when the judge handed down his sentence," she whispered. "Sully managed to get close to me and whispered in my ear that he'd get me, that one way or another, I'd pay for what I did to him."

"But no more threats after that?"

"None that I can prove." She glanced up. "However, for the last seven years, I've had this house broken into. My tires slashed. My car vandalized twice." She wiggled her fingers. "The only people in this town who don't like me are Sully, Tim, and Carl."

Blaze pulled out a chair and sat. He took her hand. "Before the rape, did they have issues with you?"

"Sully did," she said.

"Why?"

She sighed. She'd left this part out of the story and while it had no bearing, it still made her feel like she was partially at fault. She knew that wasn't true. Far from it. The therapist told her that it was normal to feel that way, but rejection for a rapist took a whole different meaning from a normal person. "Sully's the kind of man who thinks he can have any woman. And truthfully, he can be charming. He's got swagger and he's handsome. When he wants someone, he goes after them with all he's got and he wanted me."

"Well, damn. Why didn't you tell me that before?"

"I don't know," she said softly. "I never went out with the asshole. He's a ladies' man and not my type. The problem is, Sully doesn't take no for an answer and he kept trying to get me to go on a date. He pulled out all the stops and I kept on saying no. At first, I was nice, but then I got nasty."

"How nasty?"

"I told him, in public, that I would never go out with the likes of him. That he was beneath me." She shrugged. "Three weeks later, I was raped."

"You mentioned that fire was set on purpose. Is there any way Sully could have known you were working and would be one of the first in the building?"

"My schedule wouldn't have been too hard to find out and as far as me being the first in, I usually am. I'm good at what I do."

"Have you ever thought that the fire was a setup? Have the cops looked into that?"

"Of course they have. No stone has been left unturned. Everyone believes those three are responsible. But those assholes have alibis and nothing can be proven."

"How did you end up in that room alone?"

"Greg and I went into the house. We cleared the kitchen and thought we heard a voice in that back room. Greg thought he saw movement in another section of the house. We got permission to split because the fire was under control. When that beam came down and the flames got to be too much for me to handle, I didn't have time to do anything but escape. I figured my best bet was to get out and radio once on the other side, but that never happened."

"So, for seven years these dicks have been planning something and what has this Weston guy and the rest of the cops in this town been doing with this fucking case?"

"Trying to figure out what that plan is," she said.

He slammed his fist on the table and stood, raking his hand across the top of his head. "Jesus Christ, Pandora. You should have told me all of this from the start, or did you forget that I was training to be an MP before I moved over to the Marine Raiders."

"I didn't know you were with the Raiders," she said.

"Not the point. I was Military Police first. And I was damn good at that job. I'm also highly skilled in intelligence and covert operations. I need to be involved with more than being your bodyguard. We can't play defense on this. If we do that, you're a goddamned sitting duck." He waved his hand over her phone. "Call that Weston fellow and tell him to get his ass over here, now. I want to have a word with him."

"Trust me, Weston is doing—"

"Just do it, Pandora. Or I will call the police station myself." He planted his hands on his hips.

All she could do was stare at the button on his jeans, which wasn't fascinated.

Talk about inappropriate.

Then again, Greg used to tell her she used sex to avoid emotional topics, which was true.

"Fine." She tapped the screen, pulling up Weston's number.

"Put it on speaker," Blaze bellowed.

She did as instructed. It rang twice.

"Hey, Pandora. How are you holding up?" Weston asked.

"Oh, I'm just ducky, how are you?"

"Well, I'm sitting in front of Tim's place as he prepares for a party, that fucking twit. I can't wait to slap cuffs on him, Carl, and especially that fucktard, Sully. But Haven really wants that honor. She keeps telling me that if that prick is in her line of sight, she'll end him and I have to constantly remind her she's a cop. She can't do that. But you know how she gets."

"I certainly do and I love her for it." Pandora couldn't stop her lips from curling into a smile. "Listen, I need a favor."

"Anything for you," Weston said.

"Is there any chance you can come over? A friend of mine would like to speak to you about all of this."

"You mean Blaze Wright?" Weston asked. "Greg called me a little bit ago and told me he was in town. Interesting turn of events. How do you feel about running into him?"

Blaze arched a brow.

She groaned. "You're on speaker and he's listening."

"Oh. Sorry." Weston chuckled. "I can come over, but

I want to get someone over here first. I'm not leaving these dumbasses unattended for a single second. Right now, it just looks like they are preparing for Sully's return, but I want them to know we're watching. Even jaywalking will get them a ticket," Weston said. "Haven's on duty, so she can come sit here and watch."

"Thanks. I appreciate it."

"I'll see you in a bit," Weston said. "Before I hang up, I have one question."

"What's that?" Pandora asked.

"Should I bring over all the paperwork on the case?"

"Yes," Blaze answered for her. "If possible, I'd like a copy for myself so I can go through everything. Maybe I'll find something you missed."

"If I was a prideful man or if I didn't care so much about Pandora, I'd be fucking insulted by that statement." Weston chuckled. "Whatever I give you, remember, you didn't get it from me. That would be grounds for dismissal and I like my job. It took me too long to get here and if I get fired, I'll have your head on a platter."

"If anything happens to Pandora, I'll have yours on a stick," Blaze said.

"Oh my God. Enough with the fucking chest-pounding," Pandora mumbled. "Goodbye, Weston." She tapped the end button. "You didn't have to be a dick to Weston. He's one of the good guys."

Blaze smiled. "I think I like him."

"I just can't with you men sometimes." She shook

her head. "Make me French toast and bacon. I'll be in the family room, putting away your bed." She stood. "How was that thing anyway?"

"Awful. Horrible. I would have been more comfortable sleeping on a rock." He lifted his mug. "Tonight, I'm not going to bother to pull it out. I'll just crash on the sofa as it is."

"Whatever floats your boat." She waved her hand over her head.

"That would be sleeping in your bed with you." He laughed.

"I guess I walked right into that one." Only with Sully back in town, the idea of sleeping alone had her guts twisted in knots. She wouldn't mind Blaze's strong arms wrapped around her body all night like a protective shield. Except if she allowed that, she couldn't be trusted to keep her hands to herself.

CHAPTER SIX

Blaze sat at the kitchen table with Weston and a massive pile of paperwork while Pandora hid in her bedroom watching some stupid show about house-wives. He could hear a bunch of ladies scream at each other from the television.

"She can't bring herself to look at these anymore," Weston said, pushing a folder across the table. "And I can't say as I blame her. I had just finished the academy when this happened. I had only been a cop for three weeks. I was the first to arrive when the call came. I was also the first on the scene when Sully tried to rape Andrea. Pandora stared at these images and her own file for months during Andrea's trial, trying to find any similarity between her case and Andrea's, but there's no connecting the dots. Andrea did date Sully. And they had been dating right up until two weeks before the attempted rape. The cops were also called twice, by

Andrea, on an assault, but she changed her story each time we showed up."

"It sounds like it should be an open and shut case when it comes to Andrea."

"Not when it comes to the first few times we were called for domestic assault. Here's the report." Weston shuffled through the papers. "It sucks when we're forced to walk away, but if the victim won't accuse their attacker, and we can't get them to do it, we're left with no choice."

"Were there any other girls who have ever accused Sully of anything before?" Blaze held up the document and scanned the report. It was pretty standard stuff and he'd seen it before. However, in the military, things were different. They took assault and sexual misconduct much more seriously. If a man had been accused, even if not proven, they were reprimanded. It was a strike against them. If it happened again, it almost always ruined their career.

"Yes and no." Weston let out a long breath. "I have spent the last eight years talking to every girl I know who has ever been known to associate with Sully. I didn't get very far. But my wife has had better luck. I suppose that's because she's a woman, and considering what she went through, she can relate to them." Weston held up his hand. "But she couldn't get any of them to come forward. Not even the two who said Sully was rough with them." Weston pushed around the papers until he found another folder. "Neither woman would admit to being raped; however, they did say Sully hit them, but they wouldn't speak out against him."

Blaze pinched the bridge of his nose. The amount of paperwork this man had collected was impressive, but it added up to a whole lot of nothing. There were pieces that connected Sully to every aspect of Pandora's rape, but it was all conjecture. All hearsay. Nothing concrete. No smoking gun.

"What about the fire?" Blaze asked.

"The investigator can say without a doubt that it was set on purpose. It was started in the kitchen. Set by an accelerant. A neighbor called it in. The fire was contained quickly, but there was concern that Sully and Tim were inside, which everyone thought was odd. It wasn't a big fire, but it was early in the morning. Both their vehicles were in the garage. However, it turns out, they had gone camping with Carl and some other friends. There were witnesses who saw them at the campsite both the night before and in the morning." Again, Weston shoved more files at Blaze. "There's the witness list. I speak to each and every one as often as I can that wouldn't be considered police harassment. As you can see in my notes, there are some minor discrepancies in a few of the stories, but not enough to build a case for the possibility that Sully left that campsite. If I can do that, I might be able to at least get the DA to open an active investigation against Sully for the rape of Pandora, showing that he had ample time to leave the campsite, set the fire, rape—"

"I get it," Blaze said, not needing the rundown. He leaned back and rubbed his neck. "I owe you an apology."

"For what?"

"Thinking you were a shitty cop and doing nothing to try to nail Sully."

Weston laughed. "If I were you, I'd probably think the same thing, but trust me when I say, this damn thing has haunted me for eight fucking years. I'd like to believe I'm a good cop. A decent detective. But this thing keeps me up at night." He pointed to the bedroom. "That one back there is one hell of a brave woman. I wasn't here when she moved to town. But my cousins, Ethan and Rocky, were. They said she was a hot mess. A broken girl with not two pennies to rub together. She stopped in Rocky's bar and ordered a shot of tequila and a massive amount of food. Rocky sat there and watched her eat it while trying to figure out her story. Later, he saw her sleeping in her car in the back lot."

"Jesus," Blaze whispered. "I had no idea."

"Rocky tapped on the window and told her to follow him home. He and his wife helped her get on her feet because that's what my cousin does. Of course, those first few weeks as she bounced between Rocky's and Ethan's places, they got an earful about her life." Weston arched a brow.

"So, that's how you knew a little about me. Not from Greg."

"Pandora told Haven about you one night after way too many tequila shots."

"That woman does like tequila." Blaze chuckled. "I wonder why she never told Brock. I've been friends with him for over ten years."

"She and Brock aren't as close as she is with me, my cousins, and Talon, another search and rescue man. Brock is kind of hard to get to know, but he's loosened up a bit since he got married. Although he's still a bit aloof."

"Yeah. That's true and I haven't really spoken to him that much in the last few years."

"However, he's very involved in this case." Weston tapped his finger on the stacks of paper. "He works with all of us to track down leads. He helps keep a watchful eye over Pandora and what Tim and Carl are up to. I spoke to him a little bit ago as we've all got a schedule. Unfortunately, there is only so much my department can do, legally."

"I chatted with him right before you came over." Blaze rolled his neck. "He informed me that Sully should be rolling into town right about now."

Weston lifted his phone and waved it. "My wife said he's already here. Nothing to report. Just hanging out at his home with his brother, Carl, and a few other friends."

"That only means that they are sitting around a table, discussing their next move."

"Trust me. I'm aware."

Blaze stared at the folder on the table that he'd been dreading opening. But he needed to. He had to read the reports. To understand the exact nature of the crime. He lifted it from the table.

Weston grabbed his wrist. "I need to warn you that those will enrage you."

"I'm already there. I'm just really good at keeping that demon in a bottle." God, he prayed he'd be able to continue to. He flipped it open and swallowed. Hard. An image of an unrecognizable Pandora stared back at him. Her face was so badly beaten her eyes were swollen shut. Her lips were twice their normal size. It was amazing there was no scarring left on her face. "My God," he whispered. Tentatively, he traced the picture with his finger. So many what-ifs filled his brain. Logically, he knew he couldn't have prevented this. It wasn't his fault. But if he hadn't... He wouldn't finish that train of thought.

What was done was done.

Regret filled his soul.

And love filled his heart.

He'd never stopped loving her. Not for one single second. For twenty years he carried a torch for Pandora. He could lie to his ex-wife. To their marriage counselor. To the entire world.

But he couldn't lie to himself.

He flipped the page. Image after image burned into his brain. He scanned the police report, signed by

Weston. It was all so professional, and yet Blaze could read between the lines.

Weston had been deeply affected.

God bless that man.

He closed the file and flattened his hands on the table.

"You all right?"

"Absolutely not," Blaze said. "What's your plan?"

"Official? Or unofficial?"

"Both," Blaze said.

"Officially, I keep doing the same tired shit as always. I interview people. I talk to women Sully had relationships with. I try to find the loophole. Or even a mistake in the police work I did. Anything that will crack this case," Weston said. "Unofficially, well, my cousins, Ethan and Rocky, along with Talon and Brock want to set up a sting." Weston lowered his chin. "They've kept me out of the loop because I'm a cop and some of it won't be legal. But I know what it would look like and I can't say I wouldn't be on board."

"Why hasn't Brock said anything to me?" But Blaze already knew the answer to that. However, he did want to hear if Weston would be honest or not.

"I can only guess, because again, they aren't including me in the plan. They don't want to get me fired. But they do want me as backup when the shit hits the fan or they need my handcuffs, but they would also need to run it by Pandora, and Greg has kind of put a stop to that. He doesn't want her involved. He wants to find another way. So, for now, from what I can gather, they are still in the wargaming stages."

Blaze rubbed his chin. "They want to use Pandora as bait."

"They haven't come out and said that."

"I might have known Pandora twenty years ago. We were madly in love for over a year, but that was then. This is now." Blaze slowly rose and paced in the small kitchen. "Greg was her husband. He was with her when this happened and I totally understand why he wouldn't want them to do this. I don't want to put her in the line of fire. But is Greg's reasoning out of a sense of duty and protection? Out of having been in love with her and still caring for her? Or is it because he doesn't think she can handle it?"

"Both," Weston said. "I've known Pandora for as long as I've lived in Fallport. She's strong. And brave. And as much as she acts like a tough cookie and can handle anything life throws at her, this changed her. For that first year after the rape, she was a shell of a woman. Afraid of her own shadow. Greg was worried she wouldn't even be able to go back to fighting fires. It wasn't until Sully went to prison that she was able to slowly put her life back together." Weston stood, adjusting his holster. "Once we got news of Sully's release date, Pandora started retreating. It's subtle. Most don't notice it. But Haven does. Pandora's never going to be able to completely live again until that man is behind bars." Weston waved his hand across the table. "This isn't going to put him there, but I'm kind of with Greg on this one. I don't believe using Pandora as bait is the right way to go. But honestly, that's up to her."

"I don't want anyone asking her until I've had a chance to speak to your cousins and Brock about this," Blaze said. "I'll reach out to Brock. Would you mind giving me Rocky and Ethan's contact info?"

"I'll do you one better." Weston nodded. "I'll arrange for Haven to come over tonight and spend time with Pandora. Not only is she a good cop and Pandora will be safe, but she's one of Pandora's best friends. That way you, my cousins, and Brock can have a sit-down."

"What about you?"

"I can't be involved," Weston said. "Besides, I have a little one at home who will need her father's attention." Weston glanced at his watch. "I need to get back out there. Call me if you need anything at all."

"Thanks." Blaze stretched out his arm. "I appreciate the candor."

"Take care of her. I know you two have some history, but she's always spoken highly of you."

Blaze nodded, walking Weston to the door.

Once Weston left, Blaze made sure he locked up. He leaned against the wall and rubbed his temples. Using Pandora as bait was about the craziest idea he'd ever heard.

But it was the only thing that made sense to end the madness.

He strolled through the family room and kitchen, peeking into the bedroom. Pandora lay on her side, with her hands tucked under her cheek, her eyes closed. He couldn't imagine what thoughts had been going on inside her mind while he and Weston went through her file.

She probably felt as though she were being raped all over again, but this time by her friends.

Quietly, he tiptoed into the room and eased onto the bed. The women on the television were still yelling at each other. His ex-wife used to love these kinds of shows and he never understood why. He lifted the remote and found a hockey game.

Pandora shifted, stretching her legs and arms. "How long have I been sleeping?"

"I don't know. A half hour maybe."

"Where's Weston?"

"He just left."

She snuggled up beside him, draping her arm over his chest and her leg over his thigh.

It was a sensation he shouldn't welcome, but he did as he wrapped his arm around her, pulling her close. She needed comfort and he could at least give that to her.

"He's a good man and you're lucky to have such good friends." Blaze kissed her forehead. "He mentioned that Haven wanted to come over tonight and see you. I thought it would be good for you to have a little girl time so I'll go see Brock. I haven't really had a chance to catch up with him anyway."

"Are you sure?" Her body trembled. God, he hated that she was scared. But he would be too if he were her. He also had to leave for a few hours. He had to know what these men had planned. He needed to be in the know. To understand and to make his own judgment if it was a good mission or if he should kill it.

"You'll be safe with Haven. Weston has assured me of that."

"I know." She inched closer, if that was even possible.

He rested his head against hers, taking in her fresh coconut and roses scent. It got him every time. The first time he saw her on that beach, he'd been a goner. She'd been wearing a skimpy black-and-white string bikini and he couldn't take his eyes off her. He'd been on liberty call for a long weekend and he and his brother had gone to Myrtle Beach to blow off some steam.

Axel spent it in bars getting shit-faced.

Blaze spent it in a hotel room falling in love.

It had been the most humbling experience in his life.

She pressed her hand on his chest and straddled him, lifting her shirt over her head, exposing the sexiest bra he'd ever seen.

He swallowed. "Pandora, what are you doing?"

Leaning over, she pressed her mouth against his,

kissing him softly at first, but it soon turned into a wild frenzy when her tongue looped around his in a familiar storm.

He eased his hands up the sides of her body until he cupped her face, prying their lips apart.

She blinked, staring at him with a combination of lust and fear in her beautiful blue orbs.

Running his thumbs across her cheeks, he searched his brain for the right words. Any words that wouldn't hurt her feelings. She was scared. Her fuel tanks were running on empty. Her attacker had just been released and was now only five miles away. She was reacting to that and all she wanted was for someone to care for her and it didn't matter what form that took.

Only, it mattered to him.

"My sweet Pandora," he whispered. "This isn't the way to deal with all the emotions you're feeling right now."

"Don't you dare tell me what I'm feeling. You have no fucking clue." She hopped off him and the bed so fast it made his head spin.

Well, fuck. That didn't go over right.

She snagged her shirt and raced out of the bedroom, slamming the door.

"Pandora, wait." He fumbled off the bed, nearly tripping as he reached for the door handle. He found her with the bottle of tequila and a glass in her hands. "That's no way either." He snatched them up, set them back on the shelf, and sighed. "I wasn't rejecting you.

It's just that it kind of came out of nowhere. Or maybe it came out due to me and Weston going..." He let the words trail off as he glanced over his shoulder at the mounds of folders Weston had left behind.

"You don't know crap." She poked him in the chest. "And neither does Weston."

Blaze raised his hands. "Oh, really. It seems that man knows a whole lot and even knew about me." Fuck. That was a dumb thing to say. "Shit. I'm sorry. Look. I don't know what just happened, but I don't want you to do something you'll regret later."

"Because you believe I'm reacting to that." She pointed to the kitchen table. "Ever think I might be reacting to you, big fella?" She cocked her head. "I'm not the one who kept an ex-girlfriend a secret from his wife for ten years. Or from everyone in your life. You did that. Weston knew about you. Greg knew about you. Hell, half this fucking town knew about you because I wasn't afraid to tell people that you broke my damn heart and that part of me was still hung up on you." She stomped over to the closet where the washer and dryer were kept. She yanked open the drawers and pulled down a box, while he stood there scratching the side of his face like an idiot.

Because he felt like one. He had no idea what the hell she was talking about.

"And before you go and get any stupid ideas. No. You weren't a ghost in my marriage. You were right there with me and Greg. Yes. You were part of the reason we didn't work. Not because I kept you a secret like you did with Ashley, which, by the way, was a shit thing to do. But because I could never let you go. Greg thought he could live with that. And maybe he could have. However, I couldn't. It wouldn't have been fair to him, because a piece of me always belonged to you." She shoved the shoebox at him. "Suck on this for a while. I'm going to take a bath." And with that, she was gone.

"Damn. And here I thought I understood women," he muttered. He brought the shoebox to the sofa and plopped down. Tentatively, he opened it. "Holy shit." He pulled out a stack of letters wrapped neatly in a red tie. He didn't need to unfasten it because he knew what they were. She'd kept every letter he'd ever written, right down to the last two.

Also in the box were keepsakes from their time together. The necklace he'd bought the very first weekend they'd been together. It wasn't much. Only cost him twenty bucks, but it had meant something. A pair of earrings. A bracelet. A few other stupid knickknacks.

All her reminders of him and their year together in one little box.

What the hell was he supposed to do with that?

He set the box aside and made his way toward the bathroom. He tapped on the door. "Pandora? Can we talk?"

"Nope," she said.

"Come on. I'm sorry I misread the situation. I thought you were… hell, I don't know what I thought."

"It doesn't matter."

He twisted the doorknob. It wasn't locked. He stepped inside, almost grateful her body was covered by bath bubbles.

"Get the fuck out." She tossed a bar of soap at him, missing his face by an inch.

"No." He lowered the lid of the toilet seat and sat down.

"You're an asshole." She adjusted the bubbles.

"I've been called a lot worse." He chuckled.

"This is not funny."

"It kind of is." He waved his finger. "Your nipple is showing."

"Oh my God." She moved the bubbles around again. "If I ask nicely, will you leave?"

He shook his head. "Not until I've said my piece."

"Well, hurry up so I can enjoy my bath before the water runs cold."

"Look. I know you."

"Not anymore you don't."

"Yeah. I do." He couldn't sit on that toilet a second longer, so he moved to the side of the tub, which got him the evil stink eye. He wanted to burst out laughing, but he refrained. "When we were together, you always used sex to avoid emotional stress. Whenever big topics came up, you'd start ripping off your clothes, so excuse me if I thought that's what you were doing.

How the hell was I supposed to know that for twenty years you'd been doing the same thing I had."

She tossed her arm over her eyes, exposing both her breasts.

He groaned, then reached into the tub and drizzled some bubbles over them, careful not to let his fingers touch her bare skin. If he did that, the conversation would be over.

"I thought that was obvious," she said softly.

"Pandora, look at me."

"No."

He lifted her arm from her face. "I wasn't rejecting you. Being with you again would be easy. From the second I turned around and laid eyes on you in Brock's auto shop, I wanted you. I've always wanted you. Not a day has gone by that I haven't thought about you. Wondered if you were happy. If you got married and had a bunch of kids. It killed me not knowing. Axel thought I was nuts for not looking you up. He'd shove a computer in my face and tell me to find you, but I never did. What right did I have after all these years to insert myself into your life? So, me turning you down wasn't about you. It was about me. I couldn't have a taste of you and then walk away again, and trust me when I say, I'm not the same man I once was. I'm not the kind of man who can stick around. I can't give you what you want or need."

"I wasn't asking for a lifetime of love, Blaze." She palmed his cheek. "If you think I can't see inside your soul, you're sadly mistaken." She sat up, lifting his shirt over his head. She fingered his scars across his chest.

Her touch sizzled his skin, reminding him he wasn't dead. That he was flesh and blood.

"I see the emptiness in you. The coldness that's in your heart where there was once so much more. I don't know what happened to you and I suspect I never will. But what I needed was human contact by a man I once loved and perhaps will always love. I know what we had is in the past. I don't pretend to believe otherwise. And that box out there, I kept it because, like you, it always brought me back to a time where everything in my world made sense. After Greg and I divorced, I learned something about myself. That I don't need love from others. I needed it from myself. I'm not there yet because of all this shit with Sully. I don't know if you'll ever get there."

He jerked his head. "What does that mean?"

"Besides soaking up blame for things that aren't your fault, like you've always done?" She cocked her head. "You're here, taking care of me, because it gives you something to live for. When this is over, and it will end, because the people of this town, and you, will make that happen, you'll walk away. Not because you don't care about me, because I know you do. But because you don't care enough about yourself to live anymore. Tell me I'm wrong?"

"You're dead wrong." He stood. "Enjoy your bath." He turned on his heel.

"I struck a nerve."

"Nope." He gripped the door handle with his heart in his throat. He slipped from the bathroom and went right for the bottle of tequila, only he didn't open it. He couldn't.

And she was right.

On all counts.

CHAPTER SEVEN

Pandora handed Haven a glass of wine and settled onto the sofa with a short glass of straight tequila.

"Blaze is quite the handsome fella." Haven tapped her glass against Pandora's and smiled. "Weston mentioned something about if he batted for the other team, I'd be single."

Pandora laughed. "Blaze is all sex appeal wrapped in sugar and spice, that's for damn sure, but Weston isn't anything to sneeze at."

"Nope. My husband is hot." Haven kissed her fingers.

"How are you feeling?" Pandora asked.

Haven shrugged. "I want to try again next month, but Weston thinks after two miscarriages, it might be too soon."

"Maybe he's right."

"The doctor said it's fine. He told me there is

nothing wrong with me or my body and no reason we can't try again. Weston's just worried about how I will handle it emotionally. We have one healthy little girl and we're both happy with that. But we both would like to have another one." Haven waggled her finger. "Adoption isn't out of the realm of possibility. Brayden and Madison are about to adopt two older kids and they couldn't be more thrilled. But before we go down that road, I want to try one more time."

"I think that's fair, but I also know how torn up Weston was watching you go through those miscarriages."

"I know. He's a good egg, that husband of mine. It hurt him too. No matter what happens, we'll get through it."

Pandora tipped back her glass and swallowed the smooth beverage. Weston and Haven had the kind of romance that novels were written about. Haven's life hadn't been easy. Nor had Weston's. But they came together like a fiery crash and they loved each other like the moon and the stars. It was so beautiful and pure.

Much like Pandora had thought her life would have been with Blaze.

When she'd tried to seduce him, she knew he'd never fully be hers again. She could see how broken he was and she suspected it all had to do with his brother. She didn't have enough ego to believe it had anything to do with her because she could see how much love he still carried for her, and her alone. That was undeniable.

But his heart had been destroyed the day Axel died and there was no repairing that.

She hadn't wanted to be with Blaze to avoid her life. Okay, maybe a little, because she did use sex to avoid the painful things in life. But part of her thought maybe she could ease some of his suffering. Give him a little refresher course in what it felt like to be loved. To be cherished.

Boy, had he taken that the wrong way, and maybe she hadn't gone about it too well. Or at the right moment.

But that ship had sailed.

And there was no fixing what was wrong with Blaze. Not anymore. The moment Sully was behind bars, Blaze would be in that fancy pickup of his for parts unknown to slowly die.

Part of him was already six feet under.

"You look deep in thought." Haven tapped her fingers on Pandora's thigh. "Are we thinking about that sexy bodyguard of yours or something a little harder on the brain?"

"A little of both," Pandora said. "I'm nervous about whatever Ethan and Rocky are discussing with Blaze and how Blaze will react." Pandora downed the rest of her tequila and poured more. "I'm not an idiot. I know how Weston's cousins think and I know one of their plans includes me."

"They don't discuss it with me and Weston because whatever it is probably isn't legal, until they need it to be." Haven tucked one of her feet under her butt. "However, knowing what I went through, and what those boys had to do to get rid of my problem, you're right. Using you to lure Sully out of the woodwork would be the quickest, most direct route."

"Well, they spoke to Greg and threw a shit fit."

"I know." Haven nodded.

"I thought they hadn't discussed it with you," Pandora said.

"They haven't. But Greg has and he was pissed, to say the least." Haven brought her fingers to her lips, making a zipping sign. "I was told to keep my mouth shut and I have because Sully was still in prison. But now that he's out, it's not right to keep you out of the conversation. This is about you. Not them."

"Thank you for that." Pandora tossed her head back and let the alcohol burn her gut. She needed more. Not because of the topic, but because she wasn't going to be able to face Blaze when he returned.

She'd crossed the line and she knew it.

It was one thing to tell him she'd kept all his letters. Even to tell him she still cared for him—even loved him. But it was another to tell the man he was broken beyond repair.

She emptied the bottle into her glass.

"Are you sure you want to do that?" Haven asked.

"Yup." Pandora nodded.

"All right. Before you get too drunk, tell me how you feel about being used as bait. And be honest with me. I want to know the truth. Weston won't ask because as good as that man is, sometimes he has no balls when it comes to his cousins. Me, on the other hand, I'll get involved if I have to."

"I can stand up to Ethan and Rocky. I have since the day I landed in Rocky's bar." Pandora laughed. "Depending on the plan, who's involved, and how it's executed, I'd consider it. But if I'm being totally honest, that's the firefighter in me speaking. The woman who runs into danger. Not from it. The victim? The woman who was beaten into a coma and raped? That woman? She might say no and she might also panic. If I'm put in that situation, I don't know which one will come out when I'm forced into a confrontation with Sully."

"When he was assaulting Andrea, you leaped into action."

"Because it wasn't about me." Pandora took another gulp. Her mind was already fogging over from the effects. "And let's not forget what happened the moment Weston showed up. I had a major panic attack. Sully almost got away because Weston had to deal with me. If Greg hadn't been five minutes away, who knows what would have happened."

"But you did what had to be done in the moment." Haven squeezed her knee. "You're one of the strongest, bravest women I know. That said, if you don't want to do it, no one would blame you."

"I couldn't live with myself if I didn't. So, the answer is hell yes. I'd let them use me as bait, if that was the only way to nail that asshole." And she meant it. Living in fear wasn't an option.

Neither was moving.

The only problem was that she would have to say goodbye to Blaze and that was going to crush her.

* * *

BLAZE SAT in the back of On The Rocks with Brock, Rocky, and Ethan. Talon, unfortunately, couldn't make the meeting.

"Haven mentioned wanting to be home by nine, so let's get started." Blaze lifted his beer and took a sip.

Brock sat next to him, and the two cousins, who looked like polar opposites, sat across the booth.

"Listen, man, if I had known about your connection to Pandora, I would have said something about all of this before you rolled into town," Brock said. "I'm not very close to her, but these men are."

"I know. Water under the bridge. I'm just glad she's had all of you to rely on." Blaze meant those words.

"Our plan is overly complicated," Ethan said. "But it does come in phases and it will piss off Weston."

"Why?" Blaze asked.

"Because it means he will have to loosen up his patrols and he's not going to want to do that," Rocky said. "He's the best detective this town has, but this was one of his first cases as a rookie. It's been the one case he hasn't been able to close. He takes it personally that he hasn't been able to nail Sully for what happened to Pandora. Asking him to stand down will be like taking his badge away and that man worked damn hard to get where he is."

"But why would he need to do that?" Blaze leaned back. These were highly trained military men. They had seen some shit in their day and Blaze could tell they wanted Sully to pay for his crime.

"Because we need Sully to walk around in this town like he doesn't have a care in the world. We need him to believe he's not being constantly watched, even though we will be watching," Brock said. "Everyone in search and rescue is former military. Or has had training in law enforcement. We might as well have a small army at our fingertips. We've got experts in surveillance, intelligence, explosives, snipers. You name it, we've got it. But what we need is for Sully to believe he's got a chance at gunning for Pandora."

"This brings us to the second phase, which might not be an easy task." Rocky fingered his beard. "And that's getting Pandora out of the house and into the streets where Sully can run into her on more than one occasion."

Blaze growled.

"Yeah. We don't like it either," Ethan said.

"They both live in the same town. They will bump into each other." Blaze lifted his beer and took a long slow sip. He would keep his consumption to one drink. He needed to be able to drive home.

"Not necessarily." Rocky tapped his knuckles on the table. "She struggled to leave home after the rape. Greg couldn't get her to even go to the grocery store, much less to the station."

"Then after Andrea, when Sully was out on bail, awaiting trial, it got worse. She had panic attacks. It wasn't until he was locked up that we saw her out and about again," Ethan said. "She could easily lock herself in that apartment of hers and never come out and no one would blame her."

"That's where you come in," Brock said.

"From what we understand about your past relationship, if anyone can get her out, it would be you." Ethan arched a brow. "She speaks very highly of you."

"I'm still butthurt she never mentioned you to me. Or that you never told me about her." Brock shook his head.

"I'm overly curious about what was said about me." Blaze chuckled. "I feel like I'm constantly playing catch-up about what everyone knows or doesn't know."

"Let's just say that when that girl gets a little too much tequila in her, she rambles on about some Marine who ran away with her heart," Rocky said.

"And then she goes into how great you were." Ethan rolled his eyes. "But now we've digressed. If this plan is going to work, Sully needs to see her out. He needs to believe she's not afraid of him, even though she is. He also needs to think no one in this town is gunning for him. We accomplish that, and he'll start fucking with her."

"That's what I'm afraid of," Blaze muttered.

"But that's how we catch him. And not just with something stupid like slashing her tires," Brock said. "But with something real, and that means—"

"If you say letting that bastard do something crazy like kidnap her, I'll fucking lay you out right here." Blaze glared at his friend.

Brock lowered his gaze to his beer.

"Fuck. This plan is about the most insane thing I've ever heard in my life." Blaze shoved his beer to the side.

"Can you think of anything better? Because we've had seven years of wargaming and outside of murdering that asshole, it's about the best we've come up with," Rocky said.

"Give me a few minutes and I might." Blaze had been mulling through different scenarios, but he'd be damned if he could come up with one that didn't end up with him going to prison for murder.

The sound of the front door opening caught his attention, along with everyone else at the table. He glanced over his shoulder and clenched his fist.

Ethan shifted as if to stand, but Rocky grabbed his arm. "You're not going to kick him out of your bar. Let Sully and his buddies be unless they cause a scene."

"I don't want that asshole in my establishment," Rocky said with a menacing sneer.

"None of us want to see him," Brock said. "But if this plan is going to work, we have to leave him be. Just ignore him."

Blaze studied Sully as he strolled to the bar with Tim and Carl. The three of them sat down while the bartender took their order. They looked like your average everyday men. Nothing special. Average height. Average weight. Didn't even look like criminals. They all had short hair. Clean-cut. They didn't appear to be anything to be afraid of, yet they were dangerous men.

"Let's keep focusing on what we came here to discuss," Brock said in a hushed voice. "Blaze, we believe you're the best person to bring this plan to her."

"Why me?"

"It can't be one of us," Ethan said, pointing between himself and his brother. "Most likely she'll feel pressured. But then she'll get an earful from Greg on why she shouldn't. He's not down with this plan at all."

Blaze blew out a puff of air. "And you believe I'll let her think for herself."

"Won't you?" Rocky asked.

"I don't know," Blaze said. "When I broke up with her twenty years ago, I told her it wasn't fair to make her choose between me and family, ending our relationship. I'm not sure that was letting her make her own decisions. I kind of did that for her."

"Are you saying you'll try to sway her one way or the other?" Brock asked. "Because at the end of the day, this decision is hers."

"I don't like the plan because it puts her in danger. I don't like doing nothing because it puts her in danger. The whole situation is lose-lose and every bone in my body says it's better to do something rather than nothing." Blaze glanced toward the ceiling, as if it had the answers. "If anything, at this point, I'd probably try to convince her to go along with the fucking ridiculous plan, but only because she can't live here if she doesn't and I know moving isn't an option for her. She wouldn't want that. But there's a fatal flaw in the plan."

"What's that?" Rocky asked.

"Sully's not going to come after her when I'm guarding her twenty-four seven." He shifted his gaze back to the threesome. "He'll see me for exactly what I am. Her bodyguard. If this plan is going to work, he's going to need to have a reason to circumvent me. Or want to take me out too. He's going to have to come after me as well, or it won't work."

"Are you suggesting getting yourself kidnapped too?" Rocky asked. "Because he'll kill you first."

"Better men than him have tried and failed." Blaze gave Brock a little shove. "Besides, the only way to get to her is through me anyway."

"What the fuck are you doing?" Brock stood.

"Doing what my ex-wife says I do best." Blaze stood.

"Being an asshole." He rolled his neck. "Don't come over unless the shit really hits the fan."

"Fuck," Brock mumbled. "You're not seriously going to pull a stunt like you did at the border, are you?"

"That's exactly what I'm going to do." Blaze sucked in a deep breath.

"What did he do at the border?" Rocky asked.

Brock eased into the booth. "Completely different circumstances, but some chick was being harassed by a prick and Blaze got in the middle of it. He ended up with a black eye, but the other guy, well, let's just say you don't want to mess with Blaze when he's defending the honor of a woman."

Blaze chuckled. "I promise I'll try not to destroy the bar." He strolled across the room. Hopefully he could get his point across without fists. But he wasn't opposed to taking a punch. Or throwing one.

He leaned against the bar. "Hey, man, can I get a beer? Whatever's on tap will be fine."

"Sure thing," the bartender said.

"Aren't you Sully?" Blaze stared at Sully.

"Who the fuck are you?" Sully asked, giving him the once-over as he swiveled on his stool.

Blaze leaned closer. "Your worst fucking nightmare." He knocked his knuckles on the counter. "I know who you are and what you did. You're scum and I'm coming for you."

"Who the hell does this guy think he is?" Sully

glanced over his shoulder, jerking his thumb in Blaze's face.

Blaze curled his fingers around Sully's wrist.

Sully jumped to his feet. "Get your fucking hands off me."

Blaze released his grip but inched closer. "I'm Blaze Wright. Burn that name into your thick skull. Remember it. Because one day, you and I are going to meet again and I'm going to make sure you pay for what you did to Pandora."

"You don't know shit and I don't like to be threatened." Sully poked him in the chest. "Come near me again, and I'll call the cops."

"That wasn't a threat. It was a promise." He took the beer the bartender handed him. "Now, I'm going back over there to enjoy this with my friends. My suggestion to you and your pals is to leave."

"You can't tell me what to do," Sully said with a narrowed stare. "This is a free country and I'm a free man. Besides, I didn't do nothing to Pandora."

Blaze growled. Low and deep. "I'm not the kind of man you want to run into in a back alleyway. Consider yourself warned." Blaze turned on a dime and marched over to the table. He scooted in next to Brock and took a long draw from his beer.

"Jesus, what the fuck did you say? Because those dickheads are leaving," Rocky said.

"I made it clear that he would pay for what he did and that I was coming for him," Blaze said. "The rest of this town can go about business as usual, but I'm going to be in that man's face. I'm going to piss him off like no has before. It's the only way to get guys like him to fuck up and come with both barrels loaded and no real plan."

"Well, shit, we could have done that," Ethan said.

"No. You couldn't. You've all got wives. People you love. He doesn't know me from dick. He'll google me and he won't find much. But he'll know I'm with Pandora. He'll see us out together. He'll see two people romantically involved and it will burn his ass. It's the only way."

"It does make sense, but Pandora isn't going to like what you did." Rocky arched a brow.

"I'll deal with her and while we're discussing this mission, I'm running point. We're doing this my way from here on out."

"I think we can all live with that," Ethan said. "Welcome to Fallport Search and Rescue."

"I never said I was joining your operation." Blaze shook his head.

"For the time being you are." Brock slapped him on the shoulder. "Now, let me out of this booth."

Blaze stood, shaking each man's hand.

Now all he had to do was make sure nothing happened to Pandora. It would be his last good deed. His last act of kindness before slithering away into darkness.

CHAPTER EIGHT

Pandora rolled right into a solid mass. She stiffened. Her mind was filled with cobwebs. Her head throbbed. Her stomach sloshed.

"Good morning," a familiar husky voice said.

She groaned, vaguely remembering Blaze coming home last night to her drunken stupor. She pulled the covers over her head as she tried to piece together the events of the evening.

"Oh God," she mumbled.

The memory of him holding her hair back as she puked her guts out in the toilet, twice, flashed through her mind. After she was done, he gently lifted her off the floor and carried her to bed.

She glanced under the sheets.

He'd removed her clothes and now all she had on was a flimsy bra and thong.

"I'm so embarrassed," she managed to croak out.

"That's what you get for drinking half a bottle of tequila." He tugged at the comforter. "Here's some water. Drink it. You need it."

"Why are you in here and please tell me nothing happened." She sat up a little and guzzled the much-needed aqua.

"Other than listening to you snore half the night, not a thing." He chuckled.

"So not funny."

"It kind of is." He fluffed the pillow and sat up, showing off his chiseled chest with all the scars.

"You slept in here all night?" She wrapped the sheet around her body and leaned back, right into his arm, and he pulled her to his body.

Jerk.

But it felt nice. Warm. Safe.

"You asked me to. Actually, begged."

"I did no such… okay. Maybe I did." She snuggled into the comfort of his embrace. "I guess I should say thank you for taking care of me."

"You were a bit of a hot mess when I got home." Again, the man chuckled.

She poked his chest.

"Ouch." He took her hand and kissed it.

"It's not nice to laugh at someone as hungover as I am. I feel like I rose from the dead, only to die a slow, painful death again."

"I bet you do." He ran his fingers through her hair. "As soon as I got home, you laid into me about my meeting and demanded I tell you all about it. When I said we'd talk in the morning, you called me all sorts of names, then we had the vomiting issue."

"Yeah. I remember." She sighed. "I'm sorry. I've been out of sorts with Sully's return and I know all about Rocky and Ethan's plan."

"You do?"

"Oh yeah. They told Greg about it a few months back and he brought it to me, begging me not to go along with it."

Blaze lifted her chin with his index finger. "What are your thoughts on it?"

"It's so outrageous it's brilliant. It's also kind of what they did to help Haven. I mean, I get it's a tactic. And if I don't do it, Sully will rape someone else. I can't let that happen. I won't. But it's not easy to get my head out of my ass and follow through."

"I don't like the plan."

"It's not for you to decide."

He pressed his mouth over hers in a sweet, gentle kiss. It was kind and caring and she cherished it.

"I know," he whispered. "But you won't be in this alone. I ran into Sully last night and I made this our fight."

"You did what?" She jerked, which was a mistake. Her head felt as though a bomb had exploded. She rubbed her temples. "What on earth did you do?"

"I went on the offense, like I said we needed to. I pushed his buttons. I made it clear I knew what he did and that he would pay. I made him an enemy of mine. That way, he'll want to come for me too. It's the only way I can completely protect you."

"Jesus, Blaze. I'm not sure—"

He hushed her with a kiss. "Do you want to end this and live your life?"

"Yes."

"Then I'm going to keep at him, and so are you. The faster we get him to snap, the quicker this ends."

Which meant, the quicker Blaze was out of her life.

She wasn't sure that's what she wanted, but it was what Blaze did and she was going to have to let him go.

"Okay," she said.

"Why don't I go draw you a bath and make you some greasy hangover food. The guys are keeping tabs on Sully. Once we know where he's hanging out today, if you're seriously up for it, we'll go where he is, and we'll get this party started."

"Why do I get the feeling you're getting off on this."

"I take no pleasure in doing anything that causes you pain, but I will take a whole lot of pleasure in putting that man in prison." Blaze swung his legs to the side of the bed and stood, in only his boxers.

Damn.

He strolled across the room, his thigh muscles flexing with each step. He pushed open the bathroom door and glanced over his shoulder. "What bottle makes the bubbles?"

"The big one on the side of the tub. All you have to do is give it a couple of squirts."

"Got it."

The only thing she got was she wanted that man. In the worst way. Even if it was only one more time. He'd been her first. And the best. Sure, other men had been good lovers. Greg had been attentive and really good in bed. She'd never not been satisfied.

But he wasn't Blaze.

No one was.

She eased from the bed and padded to the bathroom. If he didn't want her, then so be it. She wasn't going to throw herself at him, but she'd give him the opportunity to make a move.

He sat on the edge of the tub with his hand in the water, waving it around, making bubbles. Glancing over his shoulder, his jaw slacked open. "Jesus, put some clothes on."

"No. I want in that bath."

"It's not quite ready yet." He blinked.

"There's water. And bubbles. It looks good enough for me." She raised her hands and unclasped her bra, letting it drop to the floor.

He jumped to his feet, turning his head. "Christ, Pandora. You're going to be the death of me."

She shimmied out of her panties and curled her fingers around his forearm as she climbed into the tub. "God, that feels so good." There wasn't quite enough water or bubbles to cover her body, but she didn't care. It was kind of the point.

"You're killing me here." He stared at her with wide eyes.

Lamely, she took some bubbles and attempted to cover her breasts. "Can you hand me that loofah?"

"Loofah? What the hell is that?"

"The thing hanging on the handle."

"Oh. Yeah. Sure."

He reached down, snagged it, and tossed it in the water.

"Thanks." She sat up, reaching for the loofah, exposing herself.

"Do you have no shame, woman?"

"I'm too fucking hungover to care." She leaned back.

"I'll go make some grub. Will you be well enough to eat it in the kitchen?" He planted his hands on his hips, still staring.

"No. Bring it back to the bedroom."

"You're seriously trying to kill me," he mumbled before he turned and marched out of the bathroom.

Well, she tried.

But truth be told, she wasn't sure if she'd even be able to handle him with the way she felt. She wasn't even sure if she could handle breakfast. What she wanted was some of the hair that bit the dog. However, all of that was an excuse not to leave the house. Not to deal with Sully or what happened.

Only, she had to.

Living in fear was no life at all.

She'd given Sully too much power and it was time to take it back.

* * *

BLAZE BURNED his fingers twice while making a couple of egg sandwiches. Sleeping next to Pandora all night had been both easy and difficult. Comfortable and excruciatingly painful. She'd been drunk out of her mind. Mumbling about things that made no sense at all.

And yet he understood every word.

Every emotion.

But what had sucker punched him in the gut was her confession.

It wasn't as if she hadn't said it before.

Hell, he'd even admitted it.

They both had always cared about each other. That had never changed. They had walked through life pining for the one that got away. They had never let go of the love they had once shared.

But for him, it was a love he couldn't have. Not anymore.

However, for her, it was the love she craved. Needed. Desired.

He could no longer be that man. Not for anyone. Not even for her. It didn't matter that he could admit he still had love in his heart.

Maybe if he'd managed to run into her before Axel died, but his death had changed everything.

He lifted the tray off the counter and meandered back to the bedroom. He set the food on the bed, climbed in, and found the remote for the television. "Breakfast is ready," he shouted.

"I'll be right out."

He turned the TV on to a national news channel and leaned back, stretching out his legs.

She appeared wearing only a towel.

Gripping the sheets, he watched as she pranced in front of the bed, gently opened a drawer, and pulled out a T-shirt. She yanked it over her head and let the towel pool at her feet, showing off her rounded ass.

He groaned.

He should look away, but he couldn't.

It got worse when she bent over and hiked up a tiny thong, wiggling her adorable butt.

He swallowed. Hard.

She climbed onto the bed and lifted one of the sandwiches between her delicate fingers and took a small bite between her delectable, kissable lips.

"You're staring." She licked her fingers.

"I'm a man and you've been half-naked—or naked—around me for hours. What do you expect me to do?"

She shrugged.

"You're doing it on purpose," he said behind a tight jaw.

"The invitation is there. It's yours for the taking."

She took another bite. Only, a piece of bacon hung on the corner of her mouth, taunting him, begging him to lick it off.

He leaned forward and did exactly that. "Don't be a tease."

"I'm not."

"You're playing a dangerous game."

"I'm not playing games, Blaze." She cocked her head. "It's just sex. Nothing more. Nothing less."

"When it comes to you, it's a whole lot more and you know it."

She rolled her eyes. "No. It's not. When all of this with Sully is over, you're leaving. I know that."

He opened his mouth, but she covered it with her hand. "I wasn't so drunk last night that I don't remember what I said. Yes, I still have feelings for you and yes, I always will. But you are not the same man I fell in love with twenty years ago and I'm different too. What we had can never be recreated and I'm not trying to do that. I'm living in the moment and I'd like you to consider that maybe I need this. That maybe this will give me a little strength and courage. Perhaps it's not right to use you this way and I'll understand if you say no. But it's not about you and me. Or whatever we had together. It's about getting me through to the other side."

"I don't want to hurt you and that's what I'm afraid I'll do." He lifted the tray and set it on the floor. A million and one reasons why he shouldn't do this raced through his brain. He could handle hurt. He could handle the pain of leaving her again. His heart was already broken. But could she? If he knew without a shadow of a doubt that this was truly her using him to heal, he'd have no problem with it.

Sex for him was an act of physical pleasure. One that he normally could take or leave, and lately, he'd been leaving it. He hadn't had sex in months and until he saw Pandora, he hadn't missed it all that much.

"How can you hurt me when I don't want you for anything other than a good time?" She toyed with the hem of her shirt, slowly raising it over her head and tossing it to the floor. "No offense, but regardless of how I feel, I would never want to be with a man who doesn't want the same things I do. I was already in one marriage that was lopsided. I wouldn't want it in reverse."

"It's hard to say no to that logic." He traced her jawline with his finger, running it down to one of her nipples. It tightened under his touch. He remembered the first time they had been together. It had been her first time and he worried so much he'd hurt her. He had wanted so badly for it to be good for her that he'd been awkward and clunky at first.

But she'd wanted him and she guided him through it as if it had been his first time.

He leaned forward, sucking her nipple into his mouth.

She arched, cupping his head, and moaned.

His hands roamed her body, exploring every curve and contour, his hunger for her growing with each touch. Her breath hitched as their connection deepened. He could feel the intensity of her desire, the longing that had been building within her as well.

Their lips met in a passionate kiss. As their bodies moved close, he knew this was more than just a physical act. He could lie to her all he wanted. He would even walk away in the end.

But this was more than just sex.

Breaking away from the kiss, he trailed soft, featherlight kisses down her neck, hearing her soft moans of pleasure. His hands moved lower, tracing the contours of her hips and waist before slowly sliding down, the tips of his fingers lightly grazing the sensitive skin between her legs.

Pandora let out a shaky breath, her eyes fluttering shut in response to the sensation.

Blaze wished he could be the man she wanted him to be. The man she once knew and loved.

But he couldn't.

This was all he was capable of giving her and if this was what she really needed—wanted—then he would give it to her freely.

"Please," she whispered, need and desperation echoing in her voice.

He reached down, gently spreading her lips apart, and found her swollen, aching core. Sliding his finger inside her, he felt the warmth and wetness that greeted him, and he knew she was ready.

With a low growl, he pushed into her, filling her completely, setting off a wave of pleasure that shuddered through his entire body. She wrapped her legs around him, clinging to him as he began to move inside her.

He pulled out, and as she whimpered in protest, he guided her to sit on the edge of the bed. Kneeling before her, he parted her legs wide and watched as her swollen lips glistened with arousal. He could feel the heat radiating from her center, and the sight of it made his own desire surge.

He lowered his head, his tongue darting out to taste her sweetness.

Her hands clawed at the sheets as he licked and sucked at her sensitive flesh. He used his teeth to gently nibble on her clit, eliciting a flurry of moans from her. As he pleasured her, he could feel her body tense, her breaths becoming faster and shallower.

She was close, so very close.

He continued his relentless assault on her, determined to bring her to the brink. And then, just as she was about to fall over the edge, he stopped.

Pandora's eyes flew open, her expression one of confusion and desire. "What are you doing?" she panted, her hips bucking in search of the pleasure he had just denied her.

He smiled. "Just warming you up," he said, his voice

low and seductive. He stood and pulled her to her feet. Their bodies collided, the heat between them intensifying. He kissed her passionately, and his hands roamed across her skin as if he couldn't get enough of her. He turned her and bent her over the bed. "Do you want me like this?" He had to ask. He needed to make sure he wasn't pushing her too far.

"God, yes," she begged.

With a possessive growl, he claimed her from behind, and his hands gripped her hips as he thrust into her with renewed vigor.

Pandora moaned, her body arching back into his, meeting his every deep, powerful stroke.

His hips moved in a rhythm that was both primal and hypnotic, driving them both closer to the edge.

He pushed their bodies harder, faster, their flesh slapping together in an intoxicating dance.

"Yes," Pandora whispered. Her body trembled with the force of her pleasure. Her climax exploded with such fierceness it stole his breath. His chest tightened. The room spun. He groaned as he reached his limit, filling her with his own passion.

Slowly, he pulled away and collapsed next to her, his breathing still uneven, his body still humming from the intensity of their lovemaking. He reached over and gently stroked her face, his fingers brushing against her tears. "Why are you crying?"

Dammit. He'd gone and hurt her and that was the last thing he'd wanted.

She smiled. "It's not what you think," she whispered, her voice barely audible. "It's just… the emotions of everything, the release… I can't help it."

"I'm not sure what that means." He held her close, kissing her nose.

"It's not you. Or what we just did." She palmed his cheek. "This might sound strange, but you just gave me all the courage and strength I need to move forward. More so than a bottle of tequila ever could. Or anyone else in this town."

He pulled the covers over their bodies and let that statement sink into his brain. During the two years he'd been separated from his wife, he'd had a few encounters with women. They weren't nameless, but they weren't anything other than a roll in the hay. He'd used those women for sex, or they used him and everyone was okay with that.

Before he'd been married, he'd had similar relationships. Nothing earth-shattering. No hearts were broken. Just grown-ups having consensual sex.

In this moment he was faced with one simple fact.

He'd allowed her to use him and when this started, he'd been absolutely fine with that. He wanted to give her whatever she needed. His only fear had been she'd regret it.

She reached across his body and lifted the tray to the bed. She did not look like a woman who regretted her actions. No. She looked positively liberated.

However, he had one whopper of a lump stuck in his throat.

He'd tried like hell to make that just sex. He'd done everything in his power to make it almost animalistic, which made him an asshole. He hadn't done anything they hadn't done before. And he had made sure to gauge her reactions to what he'd been doing, and she had loved it.

So had he.

Perhaps a little too much.

"Aren't you hungry?" She pushed the plate toward him and smiled.

"Famished." He took the sandwich and dived into it, doing his best to push his insane thoughts from his head because they made no fucking sense at all. The woman made him crazy. He reached for his cell. The sooner he got the plan in motion, the sooner he'd be able to leave town. "Ethan and Rocky are expecting Sully to be at On The Rocks this evening. Are you up for going there tonight?"

"I can manage that." She wiped her fingers on a napkin. "How do they know he's going to be there?"

"Because they told him I would be there." He arched a brow. "And he wants a piece of me."

"I'm not sure I want to know what you said to him."

He chuckled. "I better go shower." He kissed her, hard. Which was a mistake, but he wanted just a little more. Especially since it would be the last of her he'd get.

CHAPTER NINE

Pandora sat at one of the tables in On The Rocks with her heart hammering in her chest. She shouldn't have lied to Blaze about her tears. But what else could she have done? She needed to release him. He didn't belong to her and he'd made that clear.

Besides, he had given her strength and courage.

But not by having sex with her. He did that just by being by her side.

The door to the bar swung open and in strolled Sully with his two sidekicks. They were almost always together.

She lifted her glass and took a small sip of her tequila. She'd promised Blaze she'd keep her drinking to a minimum, but damn, she needed a little.

Blaze rested his hand on her leg and scooted his chair closer. He pressed his lips against her cheek. "I've got you. It's going to be okay."

"I want to fucking string him by his balls," she whispered.

"There's a long line of people right behind you who want to do that too." Blaze chuckled.

"He didn't rape them," she whispered.

Blaze stiffened.

Before she could defuse the rage seeping from Blaze's pores, Sully strutted across the room like he didn't have a care in the fucking world.

The asshole even smiled as he made eye contact.

Blaze squeezed her leg. Tight. Hard.

She wasn't sure if that was to keep her from bolting or his reaction to the situation.

"I don't want any problems." Sully raised his hands. "I'm just here to grab some dinner with my friends."

"Then fuck off and leave us alone," Blaze said with a deep growl. "Better yet, why don't you find somewhere else to eat."

"I'm not going to do that." Sully cocked his head. "Pandora, you're looking good."

"Don't speak to my girlfriend." Blaze pressed both hands on the table and leaned closer. "Don't even look at her or we will have a problem."

"Seriously, Pandora." Sully shook his head. "You've got to stop filling people's heads with lies about me. It's called slander and I'm getting tired of it. I spent seven long years in prison for a crime I didn't commit, thanks to you."

"A jury thought otherwise," Pandora said with a

voice more powerful than she ever imagined she'd have when faced by her attacker.

She owed that to Blaze.

"All because you fed them a bunch of bullshit. Not to mention you turned Andrea against me." Sully shook his head. "I'm real sorry about what happened to you, but it wasn't me. You should be focused on finding out—"

"I wouldn't go there if I were you." Blaze rose, inching closer to Sully.

A collective hush came over the bar.

Rocky stepped from behind the counter. Ethan appeared from the kitchen. Talon was one step behind Ethan.

Pandora swallowed her beating heart.

"We all know what happened that day and like I've said before. You will pay. One way or another. Whether it be at the hands of the law, or by my hands, I don't give a shit. Just remember what I said about dark alleys because justice is coming for you."

"Threaten me one more time, and you'll be sorry." Sully turned on his heel and went back to his friends.

Blaze eased back into the chair and nodded to Ethan, Rocky, and Talon, who went back to whatever it was they had been doing before. Blaze took a slow sip of his beer, keeping his focus on Sully.

"Do you really think all this talk about fighting him in a dark alley is going to push him over the edge?" Pandora asked.

"Yes," Blaze said.

"Why?"

"Because if we can get him to believe I'm a loose enough cannon to go after him, he'll be dumb enough to try to take us both at the same time. That's exactly what I want."

"Right. Get him to confess after he's kidnapped us both." She tipped her head back and downed the last drop of her drink. "But did you ever think that he might kill you before we ever get the chance to get that confession?"

Blaze chuckled. "Axel used to tell me I had nine lives. From my count, I've only used up eight. I don't plan on dying."

"And I didn't plan on being raped either," she mumbled. "Don't joke about death. Sully's a dangerous man."

He reached out, tracing his finger over her lower lip. "I'm sorry. I shouldn't have been so flippant about that. But I'm serious. While the plan is a little bit crazy train, it will work or I wouldn't even consider it."

"Isn't it what you'd call lose-lose?"

"Not exactly," he said. "Using only you as bait would be that. Tossing me into the mix gives us better odds. You need to trust me."

"I do, except you seem to have a bit of a death wish."

"That's not true and dying at the hands of that asshole certainly wouldn't be how I want to leave this earth." He leaned in and brushed his lips over her mouth. "Go easy on the alcohol."

"What do we do now?"

"We watch and wait until the waitress brings them their check. Then I will go have a few more words. After that, we go home. We'll start up again tomorrow. He'll want me gone in a day or two."

"You really can be an arrogant fuck, you know that?"

"I do." Blaze nodded. "Now, eat your food. We have to be ready when they are."

Pandora ordered a soda and fiddled with her salad. She did her best to ignore Sully and his friends, but it was hard not to constantly glance in their direction.

Sully would laugh and he too would occasionally steal a look at her table. Part of her wanted to pack up her belongings and leave Fallport. She could get a job as a firefighter anywhere and not have to worry about Sully ever again. She could start her life over.

But that would make her a coward.

"Hey, it's going to be okay." He tapped her knee with his index finger. "And we can scrap the plan if you want to. This is your call. It always has been."

"And do what? Because my only other choice would be to run from a life I've worked hard to build and you, of all people, have to know that wasn't easy for me to do."

"This is your life. I'm only trying to make it better."

"I adore you for that. And everyone else in this

town. I can't keep living in fear, so we keep doing this. Just understand facing him is hard as hell."

"I know that, babe, and I can't say I like it any more than you do." He pulled out his wallet. "Get the waitress and pay our bill." He handed her his credit card. "Don't get up from this table, no matter what happens." He tipped her chin with his index finger and kissed her softly. "I'll be right back."

"Blaze." She grabbed his arm as he stood. "He might not be able to carry a gun, but that doesn't mean he doesn't have one."

"Well, I've got two." He jerked his thumb over his shoulder. "And a small army." He strolled off in the direction of Sully, leaving her sitting there by herself.

Wonderful.

* * *

BLAZE LOCKED GAZES with Sully and smiled. "You should have left when you had the chance," he said.

"Get out of my face." Sully moved to the right.

Blaze moved with him. "Nope. I'm not going to do that."

"I've got no beef with you." Sully lifted his chin. "And you don't own this bar. Hell, you don't even live here. You're a washed-up Marine who doesn't belong in this town. Now get the fuck out of my way."

Blaze inched closer. "I don't want you anywhere near Pandora. Like I said, you're going to pay for what you did to her, if I have to make sure you do with my bare hands."

"I'm growing tired of your blanket threats."

Blaze raised his hands. "No threat. Just promises. Now, why don't you get the fuck out of here before I throw you out."

"Not going to happen." Sully moved to the left, and once again, Blaze moved with him, this time, letting his shoulder hit Sully's. "What the fuck do you think you're doing?" Sully glared.

"I should be the one asking you that. You're the one who walked into me."

"Are you trying to pick a fight with me?" Sully asked. "Hey, Pandora, call off your watchdog before I call the cops."

"I told you not to even speak her name," Blaze said in dark tone, inching closer, careful not to touch Sully. He needed Sully to make the first move. Or at least that's what he wanted. But if he had to, he'd toss the first punch. "As a matter of fact, don't even look at her again, because if you do, I'll lay you out flat."

"I don't know what you think you know or the lies that bitch has been filling that fat head of yours with." Sully took one step back. "But I'm not doing this with you, man. I just came in here to eat. Leave me alone. I don't want any trouble." He turned and made a beeline for the bar.

That wasn't quite what Blaze expected or wanted.

So, he followed Sully to the counter.

"Jesus, what the hell is your problem?" Sully leaned against the bar.

"You," Blaze said. "I don't like rapists. They tend to sour my mood, especially when they rape people I care about and think they can get away with it. Well, not when I'm in town. Like I've said now three times, you're going to pay—"

"I didn't rape anyone," Sully said behind gritted teeth. "This is harassment and I'm calling the cops." He pulled out his phone.

"Do it. I dare you."

"You're not fucking worth it." Sully dropped a hundred-dollar bill on the counter. "Keep the change." He nodded to his friends. "Don't even think about following me out of this bar."

"Don't tell me what I can and can't do. And remember, I'm still coming for you. When you least expect it, I'll be there and you will pay." Blaze turned and made a beeline for the table, keeping his back to Sully. "Did he leave?" he asked Pandora.

"He's walking out the door now."

"All right. Let's go." He took Pandora by the hand.

"Are you fucking kidding me?"

"Nope." He tugged her through the bar and out the front door where he saw Sully and his two friends leaning against the hood of a sports car.

Fuckers.

"I told you not to follow me." Sully pushed from the vehicle and inched closer.

"I'm not. Me and my girl are just leaving to go home."

Pandora squeezed Blaze's hand so hard, he thought she might cut off the circulation.

"Yeah, right." Sully continued to walk toward Blaze, stopping about five paces away. "You're a real piece of work, Pandora. You better stop this bullshit, or I'm filing a complaint with the cops. I served my time."

"Don't say a word," Blaze whispered. "We all know who's the liar and it isn't Pandora. Now, I'm going to get in my truck and drive away. But we're not done. Not by a mile. You fellas have a nice night."

Sully laughed. "You know, I looked you up, Blaze Wright. Yeah. You told me to remember the name. So I did. Decorated Marine. Bunch of medals. Glowing career. But you couldn't save your brother, now could you."

"You motherfucker." Blaze shoved Pandora to the side and charged at Sully. He grabbed him by the shirt collar and shoved him up against the wall. "What the fuck did you just say?"

"Oh, ex-wives love to talk smack about asshole ex-husbands." Sully laughed in Blaze's face. "Deadbeat husband. Deadbeat Marine. Deadbeat brother who let his own flesh and blood die."

All Blaze could see was red.

He cocked his fist, but a warm, gentle hand grabbed his wrist before he could swing.

"He's not worth spending the night in county lock-up," Pandora whispered. "Not tonight anyway."

"You better thank your lucky stars she was here to stop me from beating you to a pulp." Blaze released his grip. He should have known Sully could find his weak spot. Not that Ashley had any details about how his brother died, but she knew enough. And the fact that Sully had found her in such a short period of time meant he'd gotten under his skin.

Game on.

But that meant he had to get his head in the game and not lose his cool again.

That wouldn't be good for Pandora.

He brushed down the front of Sully's shirt. "But next time things won't go so well for you. Remember what I said about dark alleyways. Come on, babe. Let's go home." He looped his arm around Pandora and with his heart in his throat, he strolled to his truck.

"He wanted you to hit him," Pandora said as he helped her into the passenger side. "And you would have if I hadn't stopped you."

"Giving him a black eye wouldn't have been the worst thing in the world."

"But Weston was right there watching and he has to follow the law."

Blaze shut the door and nodded to Weston. He climbed behind the steering wheel and pressed the start button. "It would have been best if I could get him to swing first, but we don't want him in jail either. The point is to escalate and we've done that."

"How did he know about your brother or your ex-wife?"

"Ashley has social media. She's not hard to find. Even if it is private. However, she doesn't like me much. If someone contacted her and wanted information on me, she'd most likely give it if she thought it was either helping me get out of my funk or helping someone else who could be hurt by me."

"Why would she think you could hurt anyone?"

"Because it wouldn't be the first time I did." He let out a long breath. "Ashley and I had a complicated relationship. During our separation, we were free to see other people. I did. That didn't sit right with her and she never forgave me for it, especially since one of those women was a friend of hers."

"That's a dick move."

He laughed. "Maybe. But it was meaningless on her friend's part as much as it was on mine. But the problem was it happened when I came back from my last mission."

"When Axel died," Pandora whispered. "And Ashley didn't understand why you went to her friend and not her."

"That's part of it." He slammed his hand on the steering wheel as he pulled out onto the street. "I don't want to talk about this. Axel is gone. I can't bring him back. Ashley told Sully whatever she felt she needed to and it doesn't matter. I won't let him get under my skin again."

Pandora rested her hand on his leg. "Blaze, you have to talk about this. You need to get it out the same way I had to work through what happened—"

"Don't, Pandora. Just stop. It's not the same."

She recoiled and stared out the window. "That's just cruel," she whispered.

And it was, but he couldn't take the words back and he wasn't going to tell her the story anyway.

It wouldn't help her, and it sure as shit wouldn't help him.

CHAPTER TEN

Pandora tossed her purse on the kitchen table and glared at Blaze. She wasn't going to let this go. The rage she'd seen in his eyes and felt in his muscles was like nothing she'd ever experienced.

But it was the sadness that filled his soul that truly terrified her.

This wasn't the man she once knew. She'd seen him face the loss of his brothers-in-arms before. It affected him deeply. Tore through his system like a runaway train speeding down a track on a collision course with death. But he always managed to deal with the emotions. He pushed hard to get through to the other side.

The man before her now refused to even try. He welcomed the crash. He commanded it as if it were his destiny instead of something he had to go through. Had to feel. She understood how hard that was for anyone to do and Axel's death was still fresh. She knew there were stages of grief. Stages of healing from any trauma.

But Blaze wouldn't even start the process.

"What happened to Axel?" She held his gaze.

"Go to bed, Pandora." He tossed his keys on the counter and reached for the bottle of tequila.

"No." She reached for the alcohol, snatching it from his hands. "You can't have this both ways. You can't expect me to work through all my shit, go out there and come face-to-face with my attacker, and be used as bait. Fuck, use yourself as bait, if you're not willing to do the same."

"What you're doing and what I'm dealing with aren't even remotely the same thing. You're comparing apples to oranges. It's about the worst analogy anyone could come up with."

"Like hell they aren't similar and don't you dare tell me they're not." She slammed the bottle on the counter and closed the gap, poking him in the chest. "There was no way in hell I could continue living without coming to terms with this. Not with Sully out of prison. How on earth are you going to go through life if you don't—"

He grabbed her by the shoulders. "My life is not your concern." He took the bottle and poured four fingers into a tumbler.

"So, you're going to drink it all away." She let out a long breath. "Once Sully is back in prison, you're going to drive off to some town out west, hike, find thrill-seeking adventures that push your body and defy death, do anything that makes you feel anything other than what's real, and wait for death to take you, is that right? You're going to wallow in self-pity? Is that what Axel would have wanted? Your parents? What about Brenda? Or your nephews? How do you—"

"Jesus. Just fucking stop. You don't know what the hell you're talking about." He pinched the bridge of his nose. "What Brenda needs is her husband. Not me. What those boys need is their father. Not their uncle. And I can't give that to them. I fucking took it from them. Don't you get that?" He lifted the glass and downed half of it in two gulps. "Now go to bed and leave me alone."

"I'm not going to do that." Tentatively, she reached out and touched his biceps. "You need to talk about what happened to someone. You can't keep stuffing down all these emotions and shutting out the world. It's not healthy."

He jerked away, moving into the family room. He stood with his back toward her, staring out the window, slowly sipping his drink.

"It's not your fault that Axel is dead."

"You're like a damn dog with a bone." A deep growl filled the room. He set his drink on the fireplace and made his way to the front door. He gripped the handle. "Fuck. I can't even leave because if I do and that prick Sully shows up and something were to happen to you,

I'd never forgive myself." He turned, leaned against the door, and sank to the floor, cupping his face.

"I know it won't be easy, but you need to talk about what happened. You can't keep what happened wrapped in a bubble deep inside your soul. It will eat you alive and then come out in the ugliest way possible."

"Don't make me do this. I can't. You don't understand."

"Talk to me, Blaze." She knew enough about him to keep a little distance. When he'd come to her twenty years ago after a bad mission and good men had died, he paced in her dorm room. He'd ranted. And yelled. He even punched the wall, until he crumpled to the floor and cried like a baby.

But until he got to that point, she couldn't touch him.

She sat on the floor a few feet away and waited.

She'd wait all night if that's what it took.

But that man needed to purge whatever demon he was carrying, or he was going to shrivel up and die.

Or die trying to save her.

And that she couldn't live with.

BLAZE BREATHED in through his nose and out through his mouth. He wanted to run. He wanted to get in his truck and drive until he landed in California. He wanted out. He didn't want to feel anything and Pandora made him feel everything.

He dropped his arms to his knees. "Give me my drink," he said.

"So you can get sloppy drunk and avoid this? I think not." Pandora glared.

"If you want me to get through this story, I need a little courage to do it." He cocked a brow. He wasn't sure if he could. But he wasn't going anywhere. He wasn't leaving her while Sully was still a free man and he knew she wasn't going to let up. She hadn't let him do it twenty years ago, so why would today be any different. He'd loved her so much back then for being so kind and patient while he'd fallen apart after losing one of his best friends to combat. Over the years, he'd lost many more. He'd never become numb to it, but he'd learned how to process it. Though, he'd never once been able to be grateful it wasn't him who hadn't died in battle. Not even when he'd been married and had someone to go home to. Had someone who loved him.

A part of him had always felt a tinge of responsibility to every fallen man whom he'd ever served on a mission with. It was just the way he was wired. It didn't matter if he was team leader or not. He worked side by side with these men and women and it was up to him to have their six.

However, Axel's death had been so different. For so many reasons. And now his heart couldn't stand the pain a second longer. Damn Pandora for opening that box and forcing him to let it all out.

He sucked in a deep breath, letting it out slowly. He had no idea how much he'd be capable of opening up. He wanted to close himself off. To pull everything back into that small corner of his soul, hiding it from the world, and go back to being numb. But he'd give her something.

Or at least try.

"Fine." She crawled across the floor, grabbed his drink, and made her way back. "But I'm not getting you any more."

"This should be enough." He took a slow sip. "I hope." He collected his thoughts, doing his best to compartmentalize his emotions, which were all over the map. He wasn't sure what was worse. The things that Pandora made him feel.

Or the pain of his brother's death.

Both equally tortured his entire being.

"Axel was getting out. He was done with the Marines. Done with the Raiders. He had a wife. Two kids. He was tired of dodging bullets." Blaze laughed at the memory of his brother telling him his plans. Axel had been so excited about every single one. "He had a job lined up with some security firm down in Jacksonville, Florida. The Aegis Network. If he wasn't so fucking happy about the damn gig, I would have tried to talk him out of it. That mission was going to be his last. Once it was done, he had only a few weeks left. I had promised Brenda I'd bring him home in one piece, only I brought him home in a body bag." Blaze's stomach soured. He pushed the drink to the side.

"You were on the same mission," Pandora said in a soft, caring voice. The tone wrapped around his body like a warm blanket and he wanted to resent the sensation, but he couldn't.

"We'd been on the same team for about six years. It was awesome working with him. A real dream come true. The bastard saved my life more times than I can count." He lifted his shirt. "I got shot here. And here. Axel had to carry me out. I would have died if it weren't for him."

"You two have always had each other's backs."

"That mission was doomed from the beginning. It was a lose-lose and we knew it during briefing. Every man sat in that room, looking around at each other, wondering who wasn't going to make it out. At that point, I outranked my big brother. Once he started having kids, he started thinking about his mortality. I was team leader. Those men were my responsibility and I lost five good soldiers that day." He blew out a puff of air. "I made the call to keep pushing. I decided not to bail on that mission, even though I could have. I didn't know I had a mole on my team." He swiped at his cheeks. "I should have, but I didn't, and Axel died in my arms." He glanced up, catching Pandora's gaze. "Do you want to know what his last words were?"

Pandora nodded.

"He told me to tell his wife that he loved her. To tell his kids the same. To tell them we fought hard. And then that fucker told me that he loved me and stop looking at him as if it were my fault, because it wasn't. Then the asshole took his last breath."

Pandora inched closer, wrapping her arms around his body. She rested her head on his shoulder, like she'd done twenty years ago. "Can I ask you something?"

"Sure."

"If the tables were turned, would you want Axel to blame himself?"

Blaze let out a half laugh, half sob. "God, no. That kind of guilt is all-consuming. He would have had a wife and kids to take care of."

"And because you don't, you think that makes this different?"

He looped his arm around her and hugged her close. "Yes. No. I don't know. The only thing I know is that I have a hole in my heart so big I can't fix it. I could barely even stand to be around Brenda and the kids."

"Do they blame you?"

"No, and they're killing me with texts and phone messages about when I'm going to visit again."

"Ever think you're a lifeline to someone they loved?"

He squeezed his eyes shut and dropped his head back to the door. "I think about that every day, which makes it even harder. I'm not Axel. He was perfect. He was everything I'm not. He was always there for those who loved him. And even for those who didn't. He was kind. Caring. He was the best."

She palmed his cheek. "Don't you realize you just described yourself?"

"Not even close. I failed you twenty years ago when—"

"You didn't fail me. I could have fought for us and I didn't. We both made mistakes there. You and Ashley failed each other. You can't compare those. You had an amazing career and let's face it. No one asked you to stay here and help me. You made that decision all on your own. I'm sure if you dig deep, you'll find a million and one other good things you've done with your life. And so would have Axel. What you did as a Marine was dangerous. All the scars on your body show that. You could have died a dozen times. So could have Axel. You've watched so many good men fall. This one hurt more because he was blood and I won't take that away from you. But now you have two choices. You can continue down this path of self-destruction until death swallows you whole while you have no life at all. Or you can pick up the pieces and start living again. Trust me, I know it's no cakewalk. But your nephews need their uncle."

"It's not that simple. It's not like I can just flip a switch."

"You took the first step." Slowly, she rose. "Come on. Let's go to bed. One day at a time, you can work through all the grief. But you have to feel it."

"I'm not sure I want to. It's exhausting." He took her hand and hopped to his feet. "You're exhausting." He sucked in a deep breath. "Thank you." He cupped her face and kissed her. Really kissed her. For the first time since his brother died, he felt a sense of relief. His guilt hadn't disappeared. But it had eased some. The tightness in his chest opened and it filled with her love.

Dammit.

He wasn't getting out of this town now.

The only problem with that was she didn't need him once Sully was back in prison.

And she probably wouldn't want him either.

The real question was, what did he want? He hadn't a fucking clue.

PANDORA HAD SPENT a lifetime loving one man. She'd tried like hell to forget Blaze. She'd even tried to love another man, but he hadn't been Blaze.

She pulled back the covers, shed her clothes, and pulled a T-shirt over her head without saying a word. Climbing between the sheets, she snuggled in next to the man who would forever hold her heart.

He kissed her temple and wrapped his arms around her body. The television screen illuminated the bedroom. So many emotions. So many demons. So much pain.

All she had wanted to do was ease some of it for

him, but she feared all she did was bring it all to the surface.

Tears stung her eyes.

Axel had been such a kind man and adored his little brother. When she'd first met Blaze, he and Axel were as thick as thieves. Always razzing each other and Axel had given Blaze shit for ditching him for Pandora that weekend. And again the following weekend.

But Axel had given them his blessing, telling her that she had been the best thing that had ever happened to Blaze.

And now Axel was gone and Blaze was lost.

It didn't matter that she'd gotten him to speak his deepest fears. His most horrifying pain. Saying it, feeling it, certainly didn't make it go away. It wasn't going to alleviate Blaze's guilt.

Only time, space, and Blaze's ability to forgive himself would do that.

She wasn't sure if Blaze had it in him.

"Hey." He lifted her chin with his index finger. "I'm okay. I really am."

"I never said you weren't."

"Those tears tell a different story." He wiped away the few that had made their way down her cheek. "I hate that I have this tendency to make you cry."

"It's not you." She forced a weak smile. "However, I can't help but shed a few for what you lost. I'm sorry. I'm just being honest."

"I appreciate that."

"Part of me feels bad for pushing you and part of me wonders if I didn't push hard enough. I worry you're still going to walk out of this town and go someplace where no one knows you so you can hide from the pain. Or try to drink it away. Or worse. Join some mercenary group and wait for a bullet to finally take you."

He chuckled.

"It's not funny."

"Actually, it kind of is, because that was exactly my plan." He kissed her tenderly. As if he actually, truly, honestly cared about what she was thinking and feeling. "But I can't run from this any more than you could run from Sully, because if you were going to do that, you would have packed your bags long before he got out of prison and moved somewhere without anyone knowing where you were. But you don't run from your problems. You never have. You face them head-on. And I can't outrun this either. I could try, but what good would that do anyone?" He arched a brow. "You've shown me that."

"So, what will you do when this thing with Sully is over?"

"I really don't know." He sighed. "Probably start with going to visit Brenda and the boys. After that, I'll have to figure some shit out, like finding a job. One that doesn't include getting shot at every other day." He lifted her hand and kissed it. "But one thing at a time."

"Search and Rescue here in Fallport is always looking for good men with your skill set."

"So Brock keeps telling me." He traced his finger across her jawline, gazing into her eyes intently. "How do you feel about me hanging around this town?"

"Are you saying you're considering it?"

"I'm asking you what you think about the idea."

Oh God. She had no idea how to answer that. If she were truthful, she would be putting her heart on the line in ways she wasn't sure either of them was prepared for. Not after the night they had. But if she didn't at least express half of her feelings, she'd lose him forever.

Again.

"I could get used to that."

"Could you, now." Blaze tugged at her shirt, lifting it over her head. "I'll keep that under advisement." He sucked her nipple into his mouth.

Pandora arched, moaning, enjoying the way his teeth grazed against her sensitive skin.

He trailed his tongue from one breast to the other, leaving a trail of wet, sultry kisses. Pandora's hands found their way to his hair, entwining in the silken strands, pulling him closer.

With a low growl, he released her nipple, trailing his lips down her chest, leaving a damp trail in his wake.

She gasped for air as his fingers traced firm lines across her stomach, his touch featherlight and electric.

His mouth dipped lower, and Pandora held her breath, her heart racing as she felt his warm breath against her sensitive skin.

His tongue caressed her navel, sending fleeting shivers across her body. As he continued his descent, her breaths became shallower, her anticipation growing with each second.

His lips reached their destination and his tongue parted her folds and delved inside her, torturing her with the purest form of passion. She cried out in pleasure, her legs trembling as he explored her with slow, tender strokes.

"You're so beautiful, Pandora. So desirable, so alluring. I can't resist you." His hands cradled her hips, holding her steady as she writhed beneath him. With each swipe of his tongue, she shivered, her body responding to his touch with a fierce intensity.

He continued to explore her, his fingers gently teasing her swollen folds, while his tongue continued its relentless assault on her most sensitive spots. He was a master and for the moment, she was his slave.

His tongue glided over her clit, sending waves of rapture radiating from her core. Pandora moaned, her nails digging into his scalp, as every sensation seemed to heighten her desire.

Her hips bucked against his face, matching the rhythm of his tongue, while his fingers gently grazed her pleasure points. The sensations were overwhelming, leaving her panting and gasping for more.

As her climax drew near, he inserted a finger inside her, sending electricity coursing through her body. She moaned his name, her voice trembling with desire.

With a final flick of his tongue, he brought her to the brink, her body arching and trembling as the intense pleasure coursed through her. Pandora cried out, her orgasm washing over her in waves of blissful euphoria.

As her shaking subsided, she lay there, breathless and spent, her passion-flushed face turned toward him. He looked up at her, his eyes filled with fiery desire and a tenderness that sent shivers down her spine.

"I know you're not done yet," he whispered, his voice a low growl.

Without a word, he guided her onto her knees, positioning her hips at the edge of the bed. He entered her, slowly at first, but with a growing intensity that left her breathless and begging for more.

He thrust deep into her, his eyes locked with hers in an intense gaze that shocked her system. His expression was a mix of hunger and possession. His hands gripped her waist, controlling the pace as he moved inside her. Her skin burned like a raging fire that left her craving more.

Their bodies moved in sync, their rhythm becoming more frenzied with each passing moment. His every touch sent electricity coursing through her, leaving her trembling. She wrapped her arms around his neck, pulling him closer, her body arching to meet his every thrust.

As they moved together, the room filled with the sounds of their lovemaking—the soft slap of skin against skin, the gasps and moans of pleasure, and the rhythmic pounding of his hips. The intensity was overwhelming, and yet it was precisely what Pandora desired. Craved. Needed.

It wasn't long before she could feel the familiar tension building within her, the anticipation of another climax growing stronger with each passing second. She clung to him tightly, her breaths coming in short, sharp bursts.

With a sudden surge of pleasure and awareness as her body exploded in a tidal wave of bliss, she screamed his name, her voice hoarse and ragged with passion.

He pulled her close, his body shuddering against hers as he found his own release. The room fell silent, save for the sound of their labored breaths and the thudding of their hearts. They lay there, sweaty and spent, connected by more than just the physical act.

Pandora's eyes met his, filled with a mix of love, gratitude, and awe.

He pulled her closer, wrapping the blanket over their bodies and tucking her head under his chin. "I'm glad I could give you that, Pandora."

"I'm glad too, more than you'll ever know." She

sighed, relaxing in his embrace. "I don't think I've ever felt closer to someone than I do to you."

"Is that a good thing?"

She smiled. After that, there was no point in lying. "Yes, definitely a good thing. I can't imagine ever feeling this way about anyone else." Her fingers gently traced the lines on his forehead, memorizing every detail.

He squeezed her tighter. "You know, I've never felt this way about anyone else either. What does that say about us?"

"I think I'm too tired to contemplate that revelation right about now."

"All right, but I'm not letting you off the hook that easily. We'll resume this discussion tomorrow, right after your morning orgasm."

"Promises, promises." She patted his chest, snuggling in for the night. She had no idea what the future held, or even if Blaze had it in him to stay, but for now, they had each other, and that would have to be enough.

CHAPTER ELEVEN

Blaze stood outside in the park, staring at the image on his cell phone. He traced his finger over the faces of his two nephews. His heart broke into a million pieces. Images of his brother taking his last breath filled his brain. His chest tightened. He swallowed. Hard.

But he had to do this.

No matter the pain it caused himself, Pandora was right.

Axel wouldn't be proud of how he'd planned on living out his days. Or how he'd ditched out on Brenda when she needed him most.

No. Blaze had been a coward. Too fucking scared to face the truth, whatever that was, because he still wasn't sure.

He'd stood there next to Brenda at Axel's funeral when they handed her the flag. She'd wanted to give it to him, but he'd refused, which had been the right thing to do. That fucking flag belonged to Blaze and Marvin. To remember their father. To remember how brave their dad had been in the face of war.

But what had been wrong—what had been the most cowardice thing Blaze had ever done—was to drive away that very day, leaving Brenda standing at that gravesite with her two young boys. Blaze had every intention of never seeing them again.

He'd told himself they were better off without him.

That everyone was.

There was a small part of him that still wanted to believe that, but he couldn't. Not anymore. The only people who got hurt by him disappearing were Brenda and those kids. Not Blaze.

He was a selfish fucking prick for that dance and he wasn't going to do it a second longer, even though he still wasn't sure he had much to live for. Even after all he'd gone through last night. But searching out death wasn't the answer. He wasn't sure staying in Fallport was either. A part of him wanted to. A part of him would always belong to Pandora. He'd given her his whole heart and he'd never been able to take it back. Not that he'd tried. Not even when he'd married Ashley.

He'd wanted to love her like she deserved, and for the first few years, he tried.

But he loved being a Marine and he loved his memories more.

That hadn't been fair.

But would it be right to stay here while he was still a broken man? Could he ever be whole again? That was the burning question that had plagued him all night. He wanted to be. He wished he could be that man for Pandora. And he would follow through with this horrible plan to the bitter end, to ensure her safety. He believed he owed her that.

After the mission was over, he knew only one thing. He'd return to North Carolina and visit with Brenda and the boys. He couldn't see past that and he should have never given Pandora false hope that he could.

"Hey." Pandora came up behind him, curling her fingers around his biceps. "It's getting dark and Rocky just called to say Sully and the rest of his jerk friends just rolled into town."

"I need a minute," he said a little too tersely.

"Blaze? What's wrong?" She gripped his arm, digging her nails into his flesh.

He sighed. "Nothing, babe. I just need to make a phone call." He held out the image, in hopes that would be enough of an apology. "I've been ignoring them long enough. Can I have five minutes? Please."

"Of course." She turned, taking one step toward the park bench.

"Nope. Besides not wanting you to be too far away because I don't trust Sully as far as I can spit, there's no reason for this conversation to be private. I have nothing to hide from you, nor do I want to." That was mostly true. As much as he wanted to give her all that she had given him, half of him died with Axel.

She smiled. "This is your family. I don't want to—"

He hushed her with a kiss. "The only reason I even have the courage to call them is because of you. I want you to stay." More like he needed her to be by his side because Sully was only two miles away and that distance could be closed in only a few minutes.

"Okay."

Taking her by the hand, he led her to the park bench. He sat down and hit the call button, placing it on speaker.

It rang once.

Then twice.

Maybe Brenda was so pissed she wasn't going to answer.

He couldn't blame her.

"Blaze?" Brenda's voice bellowed over the airways. "Is that you? Are you okay? Where the hell are you? I've been trying to reach you for months."

"Do you want me to answer all those questions?" He chuckled.

"Damn fucking straight I do. Right after I ream you a new asshole. The boys have been begging me about when you're going to come and visit and I'm running out of excuses. I can't believe you've ghosted me. When I see you, before I hug you to death, I'm going to pop you right between those damn fucking gorgeous eyes of yours."

"I deserve to be slapped." Blaze leaned back, wrapping his arm around Pandora. "I do want to come visit, I just don't know when I can. I'm in Fallport, Virginia. I'm helping Pandora with a problem and there's no way I can leave until this is sorted out."

"Pandora? As in Pandora Maxwell? The only woman you ever really loved? The woman Axel always believed you let slip through your fingers because you were too proud and stupid to—"

"Yeah. That one." He closed his eyes and wondered if he'd made a mistake by putting the call on speaker, but it was too late for that now. He might not have said the words out loud to Pandora and he wasn't sure he could. Loving her was the easy part. That flame had never gone out and never would. It was the truly living part he struggled with. Talking about Axel had been cathartic, but the only thing it changed was that he didn't feel the urge to crawl under a rock.

That wouldn't honor his brother.

"How did you end up finding her?" Brenda asked.

"I didn't. I came to see Brock and ran into her," he admitted. "I'm hoping that this situation is dealt with in the next day or two. Once it's wrapped up and she's safe, I'll hop in my truck and head toward you. Promise."

"Don't make me a promise you have no intention on keeping, Blaze. I know you're hurting. We all are. But I can't bear to sit here with the boys and wait, so I won't tell them because, dammit, it will break their hearts."

Blaze threaded his fingers through his hair. "I'll be there. I can't promise you when. But I will call you when this is over and I'm on my way."

"What's changed? Because when you drove away, you told me—"

"I know what I said and I'm sorry." He didn't want Pandora to hear those horrible words. He didn't need to hear them repeated back. He was an asshole for even saying them. "I get that's not good enough. The only thing I can do now is be present and I will."

"I love you like a brother, Blaze, so I'm only going to say this once," Brenda said. "My door is open to you, this time. But if you don't show up, don't come or call at all. Those boys have needed you. I needed you. And you left us standing at your brother's gravesite. For all I knew, you were dead too. I won't go through that again."

"I understand and trust me, I know I've been a prick. I'll see you soon."

"You better make good on your word."

The line went dead.

He lifted his cell from his knee and tucked it in his back pocket, letting out a long breath, knowing he deserved Brenda's wrath, and more.

"That was harsh," Pandora whispered.

"Not really. Not when she begged me to stay and help with the boys. Help them get through the first month. She told me I could postpone my death wish a few weeks. That's all she wanted. But I couldn't even give her that. Instead, I drove off. I spent a week with my ex-wife's best friend, which really pissed off Brenda. I signed my divorce papers. Sold everything I owned and went to Key West before I made good on my promise to come here and see Brock." He shifted his gaze. "Which I almost didn't do."

"But you're a man of your word." Pandora cocked a brow. "You've always done exactly what you say. I admire that about you."

He chuckled. "I don't like making promises I can't keep and Blaze and Marvin deserve better than what I did. I will keep my word on that just like I will see this thing through with Sully." He stood, taking her hand. "Come on. Let's go poke that ugly bear some more so I can go wrap my arms around my nephews and honor my brother like I should have."

CHAPTER TWELVE

Pandora found herself once again at a table at On The Rocks. She fiddled with her drink, staring out at all the people. The place was hopping. Then again, it was Friday night and happy hour. Everyone came out for the two-for-one drink specials.

That included Sully and his friends.

But it wasn't Sully who had soured her mood.

It was Blaze who had done that.

All that talk of possibly staying in Fallport had been for nothing. It didn't matter that she knew he still loved her.

Blaze would leave the second Sully had cuffs around his wrists and Blaze would not return. He might not stay in North Carolina with his nephews. He wouldn't even head west and find a place to slowly die. For that, she was truly grateful.

But he wouldn't return to be with her, something she needed to accept.

They were never meant to be together.

"You look deep in thought." Haven pulled up a chair.

Pandora glanced around. Blaze was leaning against the bar with Brock, getting another round. He'd left her alone, in part to see if Sully would approach her, but that hadn't happened and she'd been sitting there for over ten minutes.

"Did Blaze send you?"

"Yup," Haven said. "He's over there talking to Brock about taking you for a stroll to the ice cream shop and how the two of you walked here."

"He really wants this to go down tonight." Pandora pushed her drink to the side.

"Don't you want this over with?"

"I do." Pandora nodded. "But I'm also scared." That wasn't a lie. Allowing herself to get kidnapped or possibly attacked again wasn't high on her agenda of things she must do. But she would do almost anything to stop Sully. And to be able to live her life without fear.

"I know. I would be too."

"How'd you do it? I mean, you faced so much coming back to this town and you could have died."

"But I didn't, thanks to all the men who are helping you." Haven reached out and took her hand. "Listen, I need to go because I'm a cop and me being here won't help move this plan along. But no one is going to let anything happen to you. Blaze will be there with you, and Weston and the gang will be following. It's all going to be fine."

"I wish I could believe that. But Sully's ruthless and you heard what Ethan found out. That man has possibly raped at least four other women. I, of all people, understand the shame that comes with that."

"So do I." Haven nodded. "And I know where you're going with this. But some women just can't come forward. We might not understand their reasons. Or even agree with them. But we have to respect them."

"I know, but if they did, we might not have to go through with all of this."

"Maybe, but then there would be a trial and Sully would still be out. At least this way, we have a better chance of locking him up and keeping him there while he awaits trial for this."

Pandora lowered her chin. "You're not supposed to know—"

"Technically, I don't. So don't tell me anything. But I'm not stupid. Weston and I know enough that will make this legal," Haven said. "Now, before I get the evil stink eye from Rocky, telling me I have to leave, why don't you tell me what's really bothering you."

"Because all of this isn't enough?" Pandora let out a short laugh.

"Come on. We've been friends too long. Talk to me."

Pandora sighed. "It's Blaze," she admitted. "When this is over, he's leaving town. For good."

"Did he say that?"

"Not in so many words, but he didn't have to. I know him. He has unfinished business when it comes to the death of his brother and I won't stand in the way of him healing that part of his heart."

"That doesn't mean he won't be back."

"He won't be. He can't. He believes he's broken and I understand why. Even if he can get past what happened to Axel, which I don't know if he ever can, he'll make his life close to where his nephews are and that's what he should do. His family is everything to him." She laughed. "It's funny. When we broke up twenty years ago, he told me he should have never asked me to choose between him and my parents. I cried for months over that. But he was right. If I had run off with Blaze, cutting off ties to my folks, I would have never forgiven myself for not being there when my dad died. How can I ask him to make that same choice? He needs to not only be there for his brother's widow and her kids, but he needs to be there in order to make himself whole again. I can't do that for him. Trust me, I've tried. I'm not what he needs. They are and I'd be one hell of a selfish woman to even ask him to stay."

"There's no reason he can't have both." Haven squeezed her hand. "The only thing I agree with is you can't ask him to choose, but if you want him in your life, you need to tell him how you feel. Letting him heal his relationships with family isn't asking him to choose," Haven said. "I've got to go. Call me anytime if you want to talk." She stood and disappeared into the maze of people.

There was no way Pandora would put that kind of pressure on Blaze. Not now. He was too fragile. Not to mention way too fucking honorable. When he loved, he did so with all his heart. And he did love her, something she felt to her core.

But in this case, love just wasn't enough.

BLAZE TOOK Pandora's hand and led her down the dark street. The hair on the back of his neck stood at attention. His senses were on high alert. He didn't dare glance over his shoulder.

"He's following you," Brock's voice crackled through the comms piece wedged in his ear.

"Game on," Blaze whispered, releasing his hand, wrapping his arm around Pandora, and pulling her closer. "Are you ready?"

"God no, but I'm tired of this whole fucking thing. I want my life back, and I want you to have yours."

He pressed his lips against her temple. "Let's duck down this street. It's even darker and no one should be on it this late at night." There were so many things that could wrong with this plan it made his head spin. It all hinged on the idea that Blaze had pissed Sully off enough that he was willing to take Blaze out with Pandora.

So far, that part seemed to be working. The chatter in the bar from the few people in Sully's circle had been that Sully wanted a piece of Blaze. That he wanted to put Blaze in his place. Teach him a lesson, whatever that meant.

"There's literally no one around," Pandora whispered. Her body shivered.

He ran his hand up and down her arm.

"He's twenty paces behind you," Brock's voice bellowed. "Tim and Carl just got into Carl's van. They parked one block away. West end of the street you're on. We're all in place. Be careful, man."

Blaze stopped in the middle of the street. Quickly, he took out his earpiece and dropped it to the ground, crushing it under his boot. He cupped her beautiful face. How he wanted to tell her he loved her. That he'd always be there for her and take care of her. But he couldn't. Not yet. Not until he could make things right with the rest of his life.

It wasn't just about Brenda and the boys. That was one part. A huge part. He needed to see them. To love them. To show them he could be there for them too.

And then he needed to feel the pain of his brother's death. To grieve.

Once he did that, he'd come back and be the man Pandora deserved.

"This is it. Sully is coming for us. Everything we've done for the last week has brought us to this moment. I need you to do exactly what we planned for. If that plan goes to shit, you need to follow my lead. I'm not going to let that man hurt you."

She opened her mouth, but he hushed her with a tender kiss. One that should hopefully tell her how much he cared.

"Isn't that sweet." Sully's voice grated on his nerves like fingernails on a chalkboard.

Blaze turned, pushing Pandora behind his back. "What did I tell you about dark alleyways."

Sully inched closer. He held one hand behind his back.

Gun.

Not surprising.

"I've grown bored with your harassment," Sully said. "Time for you to put your money where your mouth is."

"I'm not the kind of man you want to fuck with." Blaze reached for his weapon, knowing it wasn't going to help matters because he could hear the roar of the engine behind him, along with footsteps. He raised his gun.

Sully did the same. "Looks as though we're at an impasse. I shoot. You shoot. What does that solve? Why don't you put that down and we duke it out the old-fashioned way."

"You'll still lose," Blaze said.

Pandora gripped his shoulders, digging her nails into his flesh. "Someone's behind us," she whispered.

"I know," Blaze said.

"Just because you were a Marine doesn't mean dick." Sully continued to inch closer. He smiled.

Pandora gasped. Then screamed.

Her body jerked from Blaze's.

He blinked, glancing over his shoulder. Fuck. Tim pressed a gun to her temple. While he expected it, he didn't want to see it.

"Put down your gun, or my brother will shoot her," Sully said.

Blaze set his weapon on the ground.

"Kick it over to me," Sully said.

Blaze did as ordered. "You fucking do one thing to her, and I will kill you with my bare hands."

"There we go with threats again," Sully said. "All talk and no action, this one." He bent over and picked up the weapon. "Now I want your phones."

Blaze swallowed. That one did surprise him. He pulled his out and handed it to Sully, but he made sure he snagged his pocketknife in the process, pushing it up his sleeve.

"Pandora, where's yours?" Sully asked.

"In my purse." She dropped her bag to the ground.

"Tie them up and let's go." Sully waved his weapon in the air.

"Where are you taking us?" Blaze asked, keeping his gaze focused on Pandora.

She'd been quiet. Too quiet, and that scared the shit out of him. Her eyes were wide with fear. Or maybe shock.

He worried that this part of the plan had gone off too easily. Not a single hitch, except for the taking of the phones, which had been dumped in a trash receptacle by Sully, while Tim first tied up Pandora and then Blaze.

Never checking Blaze's fist or sleeve.

Thank God for small favors.

"You take that asshole; this bitch is mine." Sully grabbed Pandora by the hair and yanked her toward the west end of the street.

She gasped. Her body twisted as she stumbled.

Blaze growled, low and deep. "I promise you, once I'm out of these restraints, I'm going to strangle you until the life is sucked out of you for hurting her like that."

"You're not doing anything but dying tonight," Sully said. "You've been a thorn in my side and I'm fucking tired of it."

They reached the end of the street. Too far from where they had dumped the phones. Too far for the recording app to have picked that up to send in the cavalry.

Carl jumped from the van and opened the back.

Sully shoved Pandora inside with brute force. She groaned.

"I'll get in myself," Blaze said behind gritted teeth. Without the cell phones, there was no way to record the confession. No way to track his location.

He was flying blind.

Wouldn't be the first time.

He rolled into the back of the van and scooted as close as he could to Pandora.

"You know where to go. I'll meet you there shortly." Sully shut the doors.

Tears rolled down Pandora's cheeks. "I can't go through this again. You have to get me out of here," she said through guttural sobs.

"Shhhh. It's going to be okay. You've got to trust me."

"They're going to kill you first. Then they're going to… going to…" She squeezed her eyes shut. "I can't do this. I can't. I don't know why I thought I could."

"I'm not going to die today and no one is going to hurt you."

She blinked. "But you can't promise that."

Fuck. No, he couldn't. "Listen to me, Pandora. I know what I'm doing. This isn't my first kidnapping. I've been taken hostage before, and I survived. So will you. Have a little faith in me, please."

"Okay," she whispered.

The van lurched forward.

Someone would follow.

The sound of tires squealing behind the van rang in his ears.

He sat up and glanced out the back window.

Shit. Ethan and Rocky had just been cut off.

Blaze just found himself in a lose-lose situation. Well, he wasn't going to let anything happen to Pandora. He'd die first.

CHAPTER THIRTEEN

Pandora swallowed. She sat on the edge of the mattress with her hands and feet tied together with her heart in her throat. Of all the places Sully could have taken her, it had to be this place.

The fire.

The rape.

It all came crashing down like a tidal wave.

Blaze had been tied up in a chair about five feet away. He shifted and twisted his body. "Do you know where we are?"

"Yes," she managed to croak out.

"Where?" Blaze asked.

"Sully's old house. Where the fire happened. Where I was raped," she said so softly she wondered if Blaze had heard her.

"That's good."

Her eyes grew wide. "How is that good? Do you have any idea what it's doing to me right now? How I'm feeling right about now? This is the last place I want to be."

"People will look for us here," Blaze said.

As if that would make her feel better.

"Why did we ever—"

"Babe." He shook his head, then jerked it toward the door. "Trust me. Our fight isn't over yet."

"He's going to kill you."

"I'm not going to give him the chance." Blaze continued to shift and squirm.

"You're fucking tied up. We both are. They are in control. We are not." She slumped forward. She had wanted to believe Blaze. Wanted to believe that this would work. But how could it? Sully had the guns. Sully held the power.

"Listen to me," Blaze said, locking gazes with her. "He's going to come through that door. I'm going to get him talking. No matter what happens, please don't say anything. Not even if he starts hitting me, because that might be what I want him to do."

"Are you crazy? That death wish still active?"

Blaze chuckled.

"That's not funny."

"No. It's not. And it's not true. But seriously, I need you to trust me. I've been in this position before; you just need to let me deal with it. I've got the upper hand whether it looks like it or not."

The door rattled.

"Promise me you'll be quiet."

"I'll try," she managed. But she wasn't going to sit there and watch him die either.

BLAZE NEEDED JUST a few more minutes to work his hands free. Twice he almost told Pandora about the pocketknife, if only to ease her growing fear. But he couldn't risk it. If his back had been to her, he would have shown her, but he couldn't risk moving either.

The door swung open and in strolled Sully with a cocky-ass grin. He held a weapon at his side.

"I really didn't want it to come to this," Sully said. "I would have left Pandora alone. She's a lousy fuck anyway."

"How would you know? You have to rape women to get any action." Blaze swallowed the bile that smacked the back of his throat. He twisted his wrists, slicing his skin as he missed the last thread of the rope. He gritted his teeth and tried again. "You lured her out to this house. Trapped her in a fire. Then dragged her out a window, into the woods, beat her, and raped her like the fucking coward that you are." Blaze didn't dare steal a glance in Pandora's direction. He knew the words would slice right to her soul.

"I'm a coward? That's rich. At least I didn't let my own flesh and blood die." Sully inched closer. "Axel.

Was that his name?"

Blaze blinked. "Leave my fucking brother out of this."

"I hit a nerve, didn't I." Sully raised his weapon and pressed it against Blaze's chest. "Doesn't matter. You're going to get to see your brother again. Right after you watch me take the woman you've been pining for your entire life." He grinned.

"You touch her and I'm going to kill you. I promise you that."

"You're not going to do shit." Sully raised his weapon and slammed it across Blaze's face.

It cracked against his cheek. The taste of metal filled his mouth. The blade in his hands dug into his skin. He groaned.

Sully turned on his heel, marching toward Pandora. "You're going to watch me fuck her good. You're going to hear her scream, cry, and beg for mercy. But there will be none." He grabbed her by the hair and licked her face.

Tears rolled down her face. Her eyes were wide with fear.

God, he hated this.

"Get your fucking hands off her." Blaze worked through the last bit of his restraints. His hands were free, but his feet were not.

"The last time, she begged and begged for me to stop. She cried like a little baby. The strong, independent Pandora is really just a weak, pathetic—"

"Hey, asshole," Blaze said. "Your brother knows shit about tying people up and I told you, if you touched her, I'd kill you." He stood, waving his hands.

"There's an easy way for me to deal with you." Sully turned his gun on Blaze and charged.

Pandora screamed.

Blaze reached for the weapon, gripping it with his fingers, and used his body to absorb the impact of Sully's attack. Both men dropped to the floor.

The chair splintered into pieces, releasing Blaze's legs.

The wrong end of the weapon pressed against his chest. He threw a punch at Sully's face. Took one of Sully's fists to his head. He rolled to his right, trying to dislodge the gun from Sully's grasp.

But failed.

Bang!

Blaze gasped. A wave of nausea filled his brain. His body went numb. He couldn't suck in a breath.

Another bloodcurdling scream came from Pandora.

"That will teach you." Sully stood, dropping the weapon. He strolled over to Pandora. "Where were we?" He tugged at Pandora's hair.

"Leave me alone," Pandora whispered. Or maybe she yelled.

Blaze couldn't be sure anymore.

With all the strength he could muster, he patted the ground until he found the gun. He pushed himself up on one elbow and pointed. "I warned you, you mother fucking prick." He blinked once and then pulled the trigger.

Bang!

Shooting a man in the back wasn't his best day. But it wasn't his worst.

Sully arched, then dropped to his knees, before crumpling to the ground.

Blaze fell backward, clutching his chest. He glanced at his fingers. So much blood. Too much blood.

"Pandora," he managed as he tried to crawl across the floor, holding his pocket knife. "Can you reach this? We need to get you untied and find a phone. You need to call for help." He stared at the ceiling. Every breath he took hurt. But didn't. He tried to heave in a deep breath, but all that happened was one big fat gurgle.

Not good.

"Yes. I've got it," he heard Pandora say.

He no longer had the energy to lift his head and look up to see what she was doing.

"Oh my God. Blaze. We need to stop this bleeding."

"I know." He pressed his hand over his chest, but even he knew that wasn't going to cut it. "Let me see if I can help you out of those…" It hurt to talk.

The floor beneath him rattled.

"Brock! Ethan!" Pandora called. "Thank God you're here."

Blaze closed his eyes.

"Stay with me, buddy," he heard someone say.

But all he wanted to do was sleep, so he went with that.

CHAPTER FOURTEEN

Pandora paced in the waiting room at the hospital. It had been ten hours since they had taken Blaze into surgery. And that was six hours after they had stabilized him so they could perform the delicate procedure to remove the bullet that had hit his lung and came way too close to his heart.

The outside doors swung open and a woman with two small boys who looked an awful lot like Axel and Blaze raced inside.

"Boys, go sit over there," Brenda said. "I need to find out what's going on with your uncle."

"Thanks for coming." Pandora approached Brenda. "I'm Pandora."

"I've seen a million pictures of you and heard a million stories." Brenda pulled her in for a hug. "Any news yet?"

"No. The doctor said he'd let me know when he was out of surgery. It's been all day."

"How are you holding up?" Brenda took her hands. "I got all the details that you happened to leave out from Brock." She lowered her chin. "That was quite the ordeal you went through. I'm so sorry. But I'm glad it's over for you."

"I am too, I just wish it hadn't gotten Blaze shot." Pandora swiped her cheeks. "He could have died. He still might," she whispered, not wanting the children to hear her words.

"Don't talk like that. Blaze is a fighter. He doesn't think he is and after his brother died, he thought wanted to join him, but that's not true. Survivor's guilt is a horrible thing."

"You should know that the promise he made you, to come see you and the boys, he meant it."

Brenda cocked her head. "How do you know about that?"

"I was sitting right next to him when he made it. He might still believe he's broken. But he knew he had to make things right with you and those two over there."

"Well, that's a relief." Brenda guided Pandora to a small table in the corner of the waiting room. "He and I had some harsh words at Axel's funeral. I wanted him to stay awhile; he didn't believe he should. I called him a coward and said he was defaming his brother's memory. I didn't mean it. I was hurt. I was grieving. Axel was my world. I always knew that being the wife of a Marine meant I could become a widow. It goes with the territory. I never once asked Axel to give up his career. When he decided to do that, it wasn't for me. Or even for those precious boys. It was because he was tired of it. He'd done his time and wanted to do something different. I loved him and I never blamed Blaze, but he always believed I did. The thing is, every time Blaze got injured or shot, Axel took it to heart. Like it was his fault. So, I get why Blaze would feel that way. When I told him that, he called me a liar. Said I was only saying that to make him feel better. That's why Axel's dying words hurt him so much. Axel knew Blaze would blame himself and that's the last thing he would want."

"Those two were always so much alike," Pandora said. "I only knew Axel when we were all so very young. He was playful. A jokester. But he was kind. Always there when you needed him."

"Blaze was too, until these last few months." Brenda let out a sigh. "I get why. He loved his brother so much. Being around me and the boys was a constant reminder. All I want is for those two over there to have their uncle back."

The main doors opened and the surgeon stepped into the waiting room.

Pandora jumped to her feet with her heart pounding in her chest. "How is he? Did the surgery go as planned?"

"We got the bullet out. He's resting comfortably, but he's still on a ventilator," the doctor said.

Pandora gasped, covering her mouth.

The doctor placed a hand on her shoulder. "I'm hoping we'll be able to take him off that by tomorrow. It's more precautionary and because he was struggling to breathe completely on his own. We repaired the damage to his lung. He was lucky the bullet missed his heart altogether. It did crack a rib. Once we take him off the ventilator, we'll know more. Until then, he's in ICU. Only family can visit. And just one visitor at a time."

Brenda took her hand. "I'm his sister-in-law."

"You can go in," the doctor said. "I'll take you to his room."

"She's his girlfriend. She should be allowed to see him. Can we make that happen?"

"I'm sorry. Not in ICU. Hospital rules. Once he's out of the woods and we move him, she'll be able to go in," the doctor said. "I'll be right on the other side of those doors whenever you're ready." The doctor turned and disappeared.

"I should have said fiancée or wife," Brenda said with a laugh. "He's going to be fine. I'll tell him you're here. Do you mind watching the boys for a bit?"

"I don't mind at all."

"Thanks." Brenda strolled through the doors, leaving Pandora with two kids and her thoughts.

At least Blaze was alive.

That's all that mattered.

* * *

BLAZE WOKE WITH A START. He reached for whatever was sticking out of his mouth and rammed down his throat.

"Nope. Don't do that," a familiar female voice said. "You know the drill. You've been down this road before."

He blinked.

Brenda.

He tried to talk but couldn't.

"Can I get someone in here, please? He's awake and trying to take out the breathing tube," Brenda yelled.

Breathing tube.

Fucking ventilator.

He hated those damn things.

Shot.

In the chest.

By fucking Sully.

He remembered that.

He also remembered shooting that fucker.

Pandora. Where was Pandora? He reached for the tube again. He'd yank it out himself if he had to.

"Stop that." Brenda grabbed his arms. "I need help in here. He's not only awake, but really ornery."

He held Brenda's stare as he tried to heave in a breath. His chest burned. A beeping sound filled his ears. The scent of rubbing alcohol and other hospital stench tickled his nose. Flashes of past battles filled his mind. Every bullet that had ever entered his body he felt with a vengeance. His entire military career rippled through his system like a runaway freight train.

The men he'd saved.

And the good men he'd lost.

Axel.

His dying words.

All the fight left Blaze's body as if Axel had reached down from the heavens above and wrapped Blaze in a warm blanket.

"Well, good morning," some guy said with a stupid smile as he dared to pat Blaze's leg. "Oxygen looks good and he has been doing some breathing on his own. I'm sure the doc will be ready to remove this. Let me go get the doctor and see what he says."

Blaze shook his head, pointing to the damn tube.

"I think he wants it out now," Brenda said.

"I can't do that without the doc's order." The man pursed his lips. "Here. Use this pad and pen to communicate. If you're in pain, we can get you more meds. If you need anything else, just let us know." He left a notebook and pen on the side of the bed.

Inwardly, Blaze groaned. He could feel the machine push air into his lungs and he hated every second of it.

He glared at Brenda, pointing at the stupid thing hanging from his mouth.

"It will be out soon."

Clenching the sheets, he stared at the ceiling. He had no idea what day it was and he didn't want to use a piece of fucking paper to ask. He needed to speak the words.

"Relax, Blaze. Your heart rate is climbing. If you want that out, you need to be calm," Brenda whispered.

"I hear someone is awake," another man said. This one wore a white coat. "You gave everyone quite the scare." He pressed his little metal thing against Blaze's chest. "Sounds good." Then he glanced at all the machines. "I'm comfortable with this coming out. But I want him on oxygen and we'll monitor him for the next twenty-four hours here in ICU just to be safe. If all goes well, we can transfer him tomorrow morning."

Nothing like being talked about as if he wasn't even in the room.

"I'll be back in an hour to check on you, Blaze," the doctor said before stepping out into the hallway.

"All right, let's get this out of you." The other man leaned over the bed. "I'm going to need you to blow when I say blow. Blink once if you understand."

Blaze blinked.

"All right. Here we go. Blow."

Blaze blew as hard as he fucking could and it hurt like fucking hell. He coughed and gagged, making his chest feel like a damn war zone. He cleared his throat, but it still felt like something was stuck in there and he knew it would be like that for a while.

"How do you feel?" the man asked.

"Like death," he managed to croak out.

The man fiddled with a few things. "Oxygen is great. You're breathing on your own, but we're going to put this in to make sure." He adjusted something into his nose.

Blaze tried to protest, but Brenda wouldn't have it, so Blaze gave up. It hurt too much anyway.

"You can have anything you want to drink and we'll start you off on a soft food diet for today. I'll bring in some ice cream. That will feel good on your throat," the man said.

"Thanks." Ice cream did sound good.

"I'll be back in a bit," the man said. "This is your call button. My name is James. Ring that and I'll come running." James strolled out of the room.

"Okay, so I know I'm in a hospital, but how long have I been out? When did you get here? How did you know I was here? And where the fuck is Pandora?"

"It's nice to see you too, Blaze." Brenda took his hand and patted it.

"It's good to see you." He sighed. "But can you answer my questions. It hurts to talk, so I don't want to repeat them."

"You've been out for four days. You had major surgery because you almost died. Pandora called me because she thought I might like to know what happened. And she's currently sitting in the waiting room because the hospital has a stupid policy of family only in the ICU. I've snuck her in a couple of times, but the last time we got caught and that didn't go over well."

"Thanks for doing that. I'm sure it meant a lot to Pandora." He chuckled. "Where are the boys?"

"With Pandora's friends, Weston and Haven. Nice couple."

"They are." Blaze nodded, wishing he hadn't because his entire body hurt. "You didn't have to come, but I'm glad you did because I think I'm going to be laid up for a while and that means it would have been a long time before I got to North Carolina."

"Ya think?"

He laughed. Then coughed. "God, that hurts."

"I'm sure it does." She held up a cup of water with a straw to his lips. "So, Pandora, huh? That's an interesting turn of events. Does this mean you're going to move to Fallport?"

"I don't know. Maybe. Probably."

"Are you kidding me? That's your answer? You really are a dumbass."

"I've been awake for all of ten minutes. Cut me some slack," he mumbled.

"Nope. Not when it comes to this. You love that girl. You always have. Why can't you get your head out of your ass? She's been out there for days, sleeping in some god-awful chair, waiting for you to wake up." Brenda shook her head. "What is wrong with you?"

"A lot of things," he said. "But you don't understand. I screwed up."

"How?"

She sat on the edge of the bed, holding his hand like she'd done so many times when either he'd been injured or Axel had and they sat together while his brother healed. "I might have mentioned to her that I was thinking of staying. Then I backpedaled myself right out of town. She knows I love her, but I couldn't bring myself to say the words." He lifted his shaky hand. "She knows me. She knows how I operate. And I saw it in her eyes. She one hundred percent believes I can't commit. That if I left, I wasn't returning, even if I said I would, and she's going to let me."

"Well, that's about the dumbest fucking thing I've ever heard come out of your mouth," Brenda said. "All you have to do is tell her that you love her and ask her if she wants you to stick around. It's that damn easy, and if you don't do it the second she's allowed to see you, I'll do it for you, because Blaze Arnold Wright, sometimes you are as dumb as a doornail."

He took her hand and kissed the back of it. "I've really missed you, Brenda, but if you tell Pandora one thing, I'll call your father and inform him that it was indeed you and Axel screwing around in the men's locker room at your wedding, and not me and Ashley."

"Oh, you wouldn't dare. You know how my father is about his precious country club."

"I know. I was lectured for twenty minutes." He arched a brow. "If you say a word to Pandora before I do, the cat will be out of the bag."

"That's just mean." She leaned in and kissed his cheek. "You will have one hour after they move you to a regular room; otherwise, all bets are off. Now, I'm going to go let Pandora know you're awake and back to your usual pain in the ass self."

"Find my phone, so I can least talk to her. Please." He smiled.

"Sure." Brenda paused at the door, glancing over her shoulder. "By the way, my dad always knew it was me and Axel. It became a joke that his first grandchild might have been conceived right there in that locker room."

"You're fucking with me."

"Nope." She tossed her head back and laughed. "My dad just liked fucking with you and enjoyed making you squirm." She kicked up her leg. "I'll tell Pandora you can't wait to see her."

CHAPTER FIFTEEN

Ever since Blaze had woken up, the pain levels had doubled. He'd barely slept all night. He kept hitting that little button that was supposed to dispense pain meds, and for about an hour, he'd be in blissful heaven.

And then the cycle would start all over again.

It had taken hours for Brenda to locate his phone and bring it to him. By the time he got it, he worried it would be too late to text Pandora.

But they had exchanged a few brief messages.

Nothing earth-shattering.

Just a line here and there, letting the other know they were both okay.

She'd informed him of what happened after he shot and killed Sully. How Brock, Ethan, Rocky, and the rest of the gang all figured out quickly that Sully would take her back to the scene of the crime. Men like that had the kind of arrogance that drove them to do stupid shit.

It took them a hot minute to take down Carl and Tim. Once they heard the first gunshot, they entered the building.

Blaze had barely remembered them coming into the room. He certainly didn't remember the paramedics, the ambulance ride, or anything else.

He checked the time on his cell and for any new messages. There were none, and only eight minutes had passed since the last time he glanced at it.

Where the hell was Pandora?

He'd been moved to this room an hour ago. Granted, that was at seven in the morning and she'd been at home, finally taking the night off to get a real night's sleep. But she'd promised, once he was in the new wing, she'd be there.

He rubbed his chest, just above the stitches. They had started to itch. He couldn't believe he'd been asleep for four days after the surgery. Of course, it was not the first time that had happened. Nor had it been the first time he punctured a lung. But, God, he hoped it would be his last. He was too old for this shit and truthfully, he no longer wanted to die.

Nope. He wanted to live.

And enjoy all life had to offer.

With the woman he loved.

If she'd ever fucking get here so he could tell her,

and hopefully, she'd forgive him for being such a dumb fuck.

The door swished open and the curtain drew back.

"Hey, you." Pandora smiled as she tentatively inched toward the bed. "How are you feeling this morning?"

"I'm ready to leave this joint. I hate it here." He laughed, then coughed. And coughed some more. "God, that still hurts."

"I can't imagine what getting shot anywhere feels like, but I bet right in the center of your chest has to suck."

"You have no idea." He reached for her hand. "But I want out of this hospital. The doctor asked me where home was and I couldn't tell him. I don't have a home. I haven't had one in months. He told me I need a place to recover for at least a couple of weeks."

She eased onto the side of the mattress. "I can't tell if that's you asking if you can stay with me or not." She reached out and ran her finger across his forehead. "Because it's no problem. I'm happy to help you get back on your feet in any way I can. I owe you my life."

"You owe me nothing." He held her gaze. "But I will take you up on that place to crash. And being my nurse, but only if you promise to wear a cute little nurse outfit."

"You've always been good at defusing things with jokes, but you're welcome to stay as long as you need." She smiled, palming his cheek. "The doctor told me they think they will be able to release you in a couple of days. He said while you were lucky as hell, you're strong and a very quick healer."

"I've been told that a time or two, but I hope this is the last time I see the inside of this place as a patient." He took her chin with his thumb and forefinger. "Come here and give me a proper hello."

"I don't want to hurt you."

"It hurts me when our lips aren't touching."

"Now you're being dorky and silly."

"Pandora, I love you. Now kiss me before I go crazy." The words *I love you* rolled off his tongue as easy as apple pie. It hadn't been awkward. Or even scary. It was perfect. Right. The way his world should be.

Her eyes grew wide. She blinked. Her lips parted. A weird noise echoed from her mouth. But she didn't kiss him. She only stared at him like he had five heads.

His heart dropped to his toes.

Not the reaction he'd hoped for.

He sucked in a deep breath, fanning his thumb across her cheek. "Do I need to say it again? Because I can say it all day long. I can scream it so the whole floor hears it. I'll start creating social media profiles and make it my status if that's what it takes."

"Um. Did the doctor say anything about you having a concussion? Should I go get him? You're talking gibberish."

"We've always said we never stopped caring. Never stopped loving. I'm just putting it in some context." He curled his fingers around the back of her neck and drew her closer. "I've made so many mistakes in my life. I never fought for you twenty years ago in a way that would have made sense. I fucked up my first marriage, though that probably wouldn't have worked out anyway. I did things I'm not proud of. I hurt Brenda and the boys after Axel died. I have a whole lot of making up for that. And I backpedaled when things got a little too real with us while I was dealing with emotions I wasn't sure I was ready for. But I am now. And I'm not going anywhere. I love you. I want to be right here in Fallport. With you. Building something together. If you'll have me."

"Wow," she whispered. "That's a lot."

"I should have said it the night before I got shot. Or while we were standing in the street waiting for Sully."

"Yeah." She nodded.

Shit. He was going to crash and burn. He was too late. That ship had sailed. "If you don't feel the same way, I can stay at Brock's. That's plan B. But I had to say this. I can't keep living with regret."

"No. It's not that." She leaned over and pressed her lips gently on his in a brief kiss. "But you have two nephews who need you. You can't stay here and be with them at the same time. I understand why you couldn't ask me to choose between you and my family. I won't ask you to choose between me and those boys."

"I didn't think I could love you more five minutes ago, but I do." He kissed her, hard. With intent. It hurt like hell as her body pressed against his chest, but it was well worth it. "There is no choice. I can have both. And I will. There's a big difference. They don't expect me to choose. They love you. Adore you. Can't wait for us to be married. Have kids. Grow—"

"Wait. What?" She blinked.

He chuckled. "I might be getting ahead of myself. But North Carolina isn't all that far away. We can visit often. They can come here. We'll all be a part of each other's lives. A family. As it should be. That is if you still want me. Love me."

"You know I've always loved you. That will never change."

"Do you want me to stay?"

A tear rolled down her cheek.

Gently, he wiped it away.

"Of course I want you to stay," she whispered. "I love you."

He smiled. "You know, you're going to have to let me drive that Mustang."

"Just because I want to keep you around doesn't mean I'm going to let you behind the wheel of my most valued possession."

"We'll see about that." He groaned as he shifted to the side, making as much room in the tiny bed as possible. "Get in here."

"Are you kidding me right now?"

"Nope." He lifted the thing that held his pain meds. "I'm going to push this button in a second, which means I'll be really loopy in about five minutes. I want to be holding you in my arms when I drift off and I want you there when I wake up." He tugged her closer. "Do you have any idea what it was like to blink open my eyes and see Brenda instead of you? It was torture. I mean, I love my sister-in-law. But she's not you and you're the only person I ever want to wake up to again."

"That has to be one of the sweetest things you've ever said." Pandora snuggled up to his body, resting her head on his shoulder. She kissed his neck. "I was so scared, Blaze."

"I know, babe. So was I. But I told you, I wasn't going to let him hurt you." He kissed her temple.

"I was more afraid of losing you." She tilted her head. "After the gun was discharged, there was so much blood. You were—"

"Don't keep replaying it. Trust me, you'll drive yourself crazy. And we both survived."

"But—"

He pressed his finger over her lips. He knew exactly where she was going and his entire world shifted again. Holding yourself responsible for everyone else is too much for a single person.

Including him.

"You are no more at fault for what happened than I am for Axel's death." He brushed his lips over her mouth. "You didn't create the situation. Sully did. We simply reacted to it. And let's face it. I didn't stay to help you because I was bored. Or had some death wish.

I stayed because I love you, even if I was too scared and too stupid to admit it."

"You no longer blame yourself for Axel's death," she whispered.

"Good men die in battle." He sucked in a breath, pushing it out his nose. "I had a mole on my team. I can sit here and say I should have known, but I didn't. Neither did my CO, or any of the higher-ups. The truth of the matter is any other team leader in my shoes would have done the same thing. And it could have been me who took on that fire. It just happened to be Axel that day. I can't go on blaming myself for something I had no control over. Axel and I were Marines. We put ourselves in danger every day. He was my brother and I loved him more than anything. But if the tables were turned, he'd blame himself for five minutes, and then Brenda would kick his ass."

Pandora laughed. "I like her. I can see why Axel fell in love with her."

"She's a good woman and this is going to sound strange, but I hope one day she'll be able to find love again. She's young, smart, and beautiful." He shifted, which was a mistake. He groaned. It was deep and audible.

"I shouldn't be in this bed."

"You're not going anywhere." He raised the medication thing and pressed the button. "I need you, Pandora. Please stay with me." He dropped his hand to her leg, which was wrapped over his thigh, and closed his eyes.

His world wasn't perfect.

His soul still ached for the brother he lost. It would take time to heal that wound. But now he knew he could go on. That he'd be okay. He had a million reasons to live. Not just survive. Not just to push through another day.

But to experience life again.

And he was going to do it.

With his Pandora.

"I love you," he whispered. "I want to marry you. Have children with you. I want it all with you."

She chuckled. "Those drugs must be really good."

"Not so good that we couldn't have a little fun when I wake up in like an hour."

"You've got to be kidding."

"I'm not. You'd have to do most of the work, but my body's already ready." He raised his hand, resting it on her breast. "Mmmm, that's nice."

"You're literally impossible."

"Just in love," he whispered. The medication slinked through his system like a venomous snake. She was right. They were superb. But he meant every word and when he wasn't doped up, he'd make sweet love to her and show her just how much he wanted and needed her in his life. One day, he would marry her.

CHAPTER SIXTEEN

Blaze stood over his brother's grave. Tentatively, he reached out and fingered the letters on the tombstone.

Axel Reynolds Wright.

Loving husband, father, brother, and son.

A true hero and a friend to all.

"I miss you, brother," Blaze whispered. "A lot has happened since I was last here. You'd be so proud of your boys. They're growing like weeds and so much like us when we were kids. Respectful and yet total pains in the ass. Brenda's doing well. It's a struggle for her sometimes. I promise I'll come around as often as I can. I work search and rescue in Fallport, Virginia, with Brock. It's a great gig, although I haven't been able to really do anything but sit in the office. Oh, and I'm starting a handyman business." He stuffed his hands in his pockets, fingering the ring. "You're not going to believe this one. About two months ago, I ran into

Pandora. Yeah. Totally random, if you can believe that. Anyway, we're back together. It took me getting shot in the chest and nearly dying, but I love her." He laughed. "Of course, you've always known that. Anyway, I bought a ring and everything. I've mentioned marriage and kids to her a few times. She always thinks I'm joking. I'm not. It seems soon. Only, with us, it's like we've waited a lifetime for this. Hopefully, she won't say no. So, wish me luck." Blaze pulled his hands out of his pockets and tapped his knuckles on the hard stone. "Not the most romantic place to do this, but I wanted you, and your family, here for it." He turned and waved to Pandora, Brenda, and the two boys. "Come here."

Little Blaze and Marvin took off running like a bat out of hell. They loved to come visit their dad, and they did so every week. To them, it was like coming to church or going for a weekly family picnic. They had grown up as military brats. Lived on three different bases. Dealt with their friends' fathers and mothers dying in the line of duty until the day the chaplain came to their door.

It had been a way of life for them.

Many found that sad.

But those boys wore it with honor.

"Did you have a nice chat with Daddy?" Little Blaze glanced up at his uncle.

Blaze ruffled his hair. "I sure did."

"Can we go to the go-cart place now, Uncle Blaze?" Marvin asked. "You promised."

"In a minute. I have something I need to do first." Blaze took Pandora's hand and kissed it.

"Are you going to get all mushy again?" Little Blaze rolled his eyes.

"All you two do is kiss. It's gross," Marvin said.

"Really? This coming from the boy who thinks he's old enough to have a girlfriend." Brenda folded her arms.

"But I don't put my tongue in her mouth. That's literally disgusting." Marvin shivered.

"Hopefully, disgusting will happen shortly, so in about five minutes, you boys might want to close your eyes." Blaze reached into his pocket.

"Oh my." Brenda looped her arms around her boys. "I can't believe you're doing this—"

"Be quiet." Blaze blew out a puff of air.

"Doing what?" Pandora stared at him with wide questioning eyes.

"That thing you always believe is a joke," he said. "But I've always been serious about it. I love you. With my whole heart. My entire soul. And with my family present, ready to make fun of me, I'm asking you if you'll marry me." With a shaky hand, he slipped the ring on her finger.

Pandora held it up toward the sun. She glanced between it, him, Brenda and the boys, then back at him. "Aren't you supposed to be on one knee?"

He arched a brow. "Seriously. Is that what you want?" He sighed. "Okay." He began to lower himself.

"Oh my God. Stop. I was kidding." She grabbed his shoulders. "Of all the insane things, that is one gesture I don't need. All I need is you."

"Is that a yes?" He gripped her hips, pulling her closer.

She nodded, pressing her lips against his cheek. "One thing, though. I don't want to wait. I want to get married as soon as possible."

"We can get married as soon as we get a marriage license. Which we can do the second we get back to Virginia." He turned his head. "Boys, it might be time to close—"

She covered his mouth. "Don't you want to know why I want a quickie wedding?"

"Oh, sweet Jesus," Brenda said with a short chuckle. "I can't wait to see his expression for this one."

Pandora tilted her head. "Have you always been able to read between the lines like that?"

Brenda nodded. "Drove Axel nuts."

"What are you two women talking about?" All Blaze wanted to do was plant a wet one on his fiancée's lips.

Damn, that had a nice ring to it.

It was going to sound even better when he got to call her his wife.

"This might get awkward with little ears," Pandora said. "I hadn't planned on saying this here."

"Boys, go down to the car. We'll be right there." Brenda gave them a good shove.

They scoffed for a second, then took off running.

"Go ahead." Brenda smiled. "And don't ask me to leave because I'm not going to. This is going to be classic."

Blaze slapped his hands on his thighs. "I feel like my proposal was kind of ruined here. Someone want to tell me what's going on?"

Pandora palmed his cheek. "It was a beautiful way to ask me to marry you. I loved that it was here. But I feel like I owe you an explanation about how this happened."

"Babe, I'm so lost."

"When you were in the hospital, I never went home. Not until after you woke up. People would try to make me, but I couldn't. I'd pretend to leave, but I didn't."

"What does this have to do with us getting married as soon as possible?"

"During those first five days, I never took my birth control pills, and then you decided we should get frisky the first chance you got right there in the hospital." She cocked her head. "You know what happens when a woman doesn't take birth control and they have unprotected sex?"

It took about three seconds for that concept to smack his brain like a grenade going off in his skull.

A baby.

He was going to be a father.

Well, holy fuck.

He cupped Pandora's face and kissed her like there was no tomorrow. It was wild. Passionate. Loving. All the things that went into a kiss that told a woman there would never be anyone else. That she was the only one who mattered. Well, her and the little person they had created.

"That was not the reaction I expected," Brenda said. "I'd been hoping for shock. Maybe tripping over his feet. Falling on his face. But not that. I'll be at the car with the boys."

He dropped his forehead to hers and blinked. "You're really pregnant."

"Yup," she said. "How do you feel about that?"

"Incredibly happy. Utterly terrified."

She laughed, but a few tears trickled down her face. "Me too."

"You didn't seem surprised by my proposal, which actually shocked me. I've been hinting at it since the hospital, and you've been brushing it under the rug."

"At first, I did think you were joking, but three days ago, I saw the ring."

He jerked his head back. "Seriously?"

"You suck at hiding things. I mean, did you think hiding it in your underwear drawer was a good spot? You're great about doing laundry, but not so much at putting it away." She raised up on tiptoe and kissed him softly. "I think it's time we ditch the one-bedroom apartment and start searching for a home. One with a backyard. One that our children can play in and your nephews—"

"Our nephews."

She nodded. "Can come play ball in."

"I love you so much it hurts sometimes."

She pressed her hand over the exact spot where he'd been shot. "I love you and if we have a boy, I want to name him after your brother."

He closed his eyes for a second and exhaled. "Axel would have loved that. He always knew you were the one." Blaze blinked. "And if it's a girl?"

Pandora glanced over her shoulder. "Brenda."

"She'll hate that." Blaze laughed. "But I love it." He took Pandora by the hand. "Come on. We need to take those boys go-carting."

"Yeah. I'm not sure I should be doing that. But I'll enjoy watching you with a big thing of buttery popcorn while those two ram their cars into you because you're a shitty driver."

"Am not."

"Are too."

They could go on like this forever.

For the longest time, Blaze had thought he'd been waiting for death. But what he'd really been doing was searching for Pandora.

EIGHT MONTHS LATER...

"Come on, babe, you've got this." Blaze held Pandora's hand, gazing into her eyes.

Her hair was soaked from perspiration. Fourteen hours of labor. The last three of them were grueling. She'd been pushing for nearly forty minutes, but this damn kid of theirs didn't seem to want to come out and meet their parents.

"I need another big push with the next contraction," the doctor said.

The nurse glanced between the monitor that checked the baby's vitals and the doctor with a crinkled brow.

Blaze didn't like that expression.

Pandora groaned, shaking her head.

"Our baby's almost here," he whispered in her ear, reaching for the back of her knee, lifting it as the next contraction started. "Big breath and push."

Exhaustion filled Pandora's eyes. She inhaled, leaning forward. She moaned as her face turned red.

But it wasn't enough.

One of the monitors dinged an alarm.

Pandora fell back on the bed, gasping for air.

For the first time in a long while, Blaze had no idea what to do.

"Pandora," the doctor said softly. "The baby is in distress. I'm sorry, but we're going to have to move you to an OR and do a C-section. I know that's not what you wanted."

"Oh, hell no. You are not cutting me open," Pandora said with more strength in her voice than she'd had in hours. "I'll get this kid out with the push. I swear if it's the last thing I do."

"You've got one or two more tries, but otherwise, we've got to do this another way." The doctor glanced to the nurse. "Make the call to have an OR ready. We've got to move her within the next five minutes."

Blaze swallowed his beating heart. All he cared about was that his wife and child were safe. How that happened, he didn't care.

"Here comes another one." Pandora held his gaze. "I've got this." She nodded.

All he could do was support his wife. He kissed her temple, helping her raise her leg as she bore down, hard.

"That's it, Pandora. Keep pushing. Don't stop until I

tell you." The doctor shifted in his seat. "Check this out, Dad."

For the last few hours, all Blaze had done was focus on the woman he loved. He leaned over and watched as the head of *his child* appeared. Tears burned his eyes.

"Stop pushing, Pandora," the doctor said as he shifted the baby. "Okay. One more push."

Pandora groaned and the shoulders appeared. Then the rest of the body.

"It's a boy," Blaze whispered as his son screamed bloody murder. His arms and legs stiffened and shook.

The doctor placed little Axel Marvin on Pandora's stomach and handed Blaze a pair of tiny scissors. "Would you like to cut the cord?"

Blaze's soul was filled with so much love he thought he might pass out from it. He snipped and the doctor put a clamp over it.

Pandora hugged and kissed their child. Axel blinked his little eyes, staring at his mother, and he immediately calmed. She smiled up at Blaze as if she hadn't experienced the most excruciating thing in the world. "I can't believe he's finally here." She kissed his forehead, closing her eyes. "Not that I'm looking forward to doing that all over again, but I do want at least one more."

"Oh my God." Blaze raked his fingers through his hair. "I have no words for that."

The doctor laughed. "Not the first mother to utter those words. Now, unfortunately, we're going to have to take him for a minute, clean him up, check his vitals, weigh him, all that good stuff."

"He looks big to me." Blaze's chest filled with pride. It didn't matter to him if he had a boy or a girl.

But he had to admit, having a son and naming him after his brother and father had meant more to him than he could even express.

"I'm guessing nine pounds." As soon as the nurse lifted Axel from Pandora's chest, he started to cry again.

Blaze sat on the edge of the bed, holding Pandora's hand. "I love you so much." He glanced over his shoulder. Hearing his son cry tugged at his heart. "I love him more than I ever thought I could another human."

"You're a daddy."

"And you're a mommy." He swiped at his cheeks.

"I was wrong," the nurse said. "This little guy weighs in at ten pounds two ounces and is twenty-three inches long. No wonder he didn't come out easily."

"Thanks for the reminder." Pandora poked Blaze in the chest. "That was all your fault. I was a tiny baby and as I recall you and your brother were massive."

"I wasn't that big. I think my parents said a little over nine pounds."

The nurse swaddled Axel and brought him back, handing him to Blaze.

Tentatively, he took his son into his arms. "Hello there, little man." He kissed his son's forehead. "I'm your dad. I can't promise to be a great one, but I can promise you that I will love you and your mom with all my heart."

Axel blinked, then yawned, as if exhausted by the day's events.

Blazed chuckled, setting the child on Pandora's chest. "He's perfect and so are you." He'd spent the last twenty years searching for something to make him feel like he was alive. When in reality, all he'd ever needed was Pandora. She was who he should have been searching for and now that he'd found her again, he was never letting go.

She was his heart. His soul. His lifeline.

He would spend the rest of his life honoring her the way he should have twenty years ago.

And his brother would live on through his son.

***

Thank you for taking the time to read *Searching for Pandora.* Please feel free to leave an honest review. For more information about the Aegis Network, please check out all of my other titles!

<u>In Two Weeks</u>

<u>Dark Water</u>

<u>Deadly Secrets</u>

<u>Murder in Paradise Bay</u>

<u>To Protect His own</u>

<u>Deadly Seduction</u>

<u>When A Stranger Calls</u>

<u>His Deadly Past</u>

<u>The Corkscrew Killer</u>

First Responders: A spin-off from the NY State Troopers series

<u>Playing With Fire</u>

<u>Private Conversation</u>

<u>The Right Groom</u>

<u>After The Fire</u>

<u>Caught In The Flames</u>

<u>Chasing The Fire</u>

Legacy Series

<u>Dark Legacy</u>

<u>Legacy of Lies</u>

<u>Secret Legacy</u>

Emerald City

<u>Investigate Away</u>

<u>Sail Away</u>

<u>Fly Away</u>

<u>Flirt Away</u>

Colorado Brotherhood Protectors

<u>Fighting For Esme</u>

<u>Defending Raven</u>

<u>Fay's Six</u>

<u>Darius' Promise</u>

Yellowstone Brotherhood Protectors

<u>Guarding Payton</u>

<u>Wyatt's Mission</u>

<u>Corbin's Mission</u>

Candlewood Falls

<u>Rivers Edge</u>

<u>The Buried Secret</u>

<u>Its In His Kiss</u>

<u>Lips Of An Angel</u>

<u>Kisses Sweeter than Wine</u>

<u>A Little Bit Whiskey</u>

It's all in the Whiskey

<u>Johnnie Walker</u>

<u>Georgia Moon</u>

Jack Daniels

Jim Beam

Whiskey Sour

Whiskey Cobbler

Whiskey Smash

Irish Whiskey

The Monroes

Color Me Yours

Color Me Smart

Color Me Free

Color Me Lucky

Color Me Ice

Color Me Home

Search and Rescue

Protecting Ainsley

Protecting Clover

Protecting Olympia

Protecting Freedom

Protecting Princess

Protecting Marlowe

DELTA FORCE-NEXT GENERATION

Shielding Jolene

Rex's Honor

Kent's Honor

Aegis Network Short Stories

Max & Milian

A Christmas Miracle

Spinning Wheels

Holiday's Vacation

The Brotherhood Protectors

Out of the Wild

Rough Justice

Rough Around The Edges

Rough Ride

Rough Edge

Rough Beauty

The Brotherhood Protectors

The Saving Series

Saving Love

Saving Magnolia

Saving Leather

Hot Hunks

Cove's Blind Date Blows Up

My Everyday Hero – Ledger

The New Order

ABOUT THE AUTHOR

Jen Talty is the *USA Today* Bestselling Author of Contemporary Romance, Romantic Suspense, and Paranormal Romance. In the fall of 2020, her short story was selected and featured in a 1001 Dark Nights Anthology.

Regardless of the genre, her goal is to take you on a ride that will leave you floating under the sun with warmth in your heart. She writes stories about broken heroes and heroines who aren't necessarily looking for romance, but in the end, they find the kind of love books are written about :).

She first started writing while carting her kids to one hockey rink after the other, averaging 170 games per year between 3 kids in 2 countries and 5 states. Her first book, IN TWO WEEKS was originally published in 2007. In 2010 she helped form a publishing company (Cool Gus Publishing) with *NY Times* Bestselling Author Bob Mayer where she ran the technical side of the business through 2016.

Jen is currently enjoying the next phase of her life…the empty nester! She and her husband reside in Jupiter, Florida.

Grab a glass of vino, kick back, relax, and let the romance roll in…

Sign up for my Newsletter (https://dl.bookfunnel.com/82gm8b9k4y) where I often give away free books before publication.

Join my private Facebook group (https://www.facebook.com/groups/191706547909047/) where I post exclusive excerpts and discuss all things murder and love!

Never miss a new release. Follow me on Amazon:amazon.com/author/jentalty

And on Bookbub: bookbub.com/authors/jen-talty

There are many more books in this fan fiction world than listed here, for an up-to-date list go to www.AcesPress.com

You can also visit our Amazon page at:
http://www.amazon.com/author/operationalpha

Special Forces: Operation Alpha World

Christie Adams: Charity's Heart
Elizabella Baker: Challenging Luke
Linzi Baxter: Dangerous Rescue
Misha Blake: Flash
Anna Blakely: Rescuing Gracelynn
Julia Bright: Saving Lorelei
Cara Carnes: Protecting Mari
Kendra Mei Chailyn: Beast
Melissa Kay Clarke: Rescuing Annabeth
Gia Cobie: Saved from Revenge
Samantha Cole: Handling Haven
KaLyn Cooper: Spring Unveiled
Jordan Dane: Redemption for Avery
D.M. Earl: Claire's Guardian
Riley Edwards: Protecting Olivia
Dorothy Ewels: Knight's Queen
Lila Ferrari: Protecting Joy
Nicole Flockton: Protecting Maria
Amy Gamet: Guarded by the SEAL
Lea Griffith: Finding Ava
Desiree Holt: Protecting Maddie

Tyler Anne Snell: Cowboy Heat
Dee Stewart: Fighting for Brielle
Lynne St. James: SEAL's Spitfire
Bella Stone: Rexar
Jen Talty: Protecting Ainsley
Reina Torres, Rescuing Hi'ilani
LJ Vickery: Circus Comes to Town
R. C. Wynne: Shadows Renewed

Delta Team Three Series
Lori Ryan: Nori's Delta
Becca Jameson: Destiny's Delta
Lynne St James, Gwen's Delta
Elle James: Ivy's Delta
Riley Edwards: Hope's Delta

Police and Fire: Operation Alpha World
Freya Barker: Burning for Autumn
B.P. Beth: Scott
Jane Blythe: Salvaging Marigold
Julia Bright: Justice for Amber
Gia Cobie: Saved from Revenge
Hadley Finn: Exton
Danielle M. Haas: Crossroads of Betrayal
Deanndra Hall: Shelter for Sharla
Jenna Harte: Dead But Not Forgotten
India Kells: Game Master
Amber Kuhlman: Protecting Paisley
Reina Torres: Justice for Sloane

Aubree Valentine, Justice for Danielle
Maddie Wade: Finding English

Tarpley VFD Series
Silver James, Fighting for Elena
Deanndra Hall, Fighting for Carly
Haven Rose, Fighting for Calliope
MJ Nightingale, Fighting for Jemma
TL Reeve, Fighting for Brittney
Nicole Flockton, Fighting for Nadia

Deserving Maisy (Oct 2024)
Deserving Ryleigh (Jan 2025)

SEAL of Protection: Alliance Series

Protecting Remi
Protecting Wren (Nov 2024)
Protecting Josie (Mar 2025)
Protecting Maggie (TBA)
Protecting Addison (TBA)
Protecting Kelli (TBA)
Protecting Bree (TBA)

Delta Team Two Series

Shielding Gillian
Shielding Kinley
Shielding Aspen
Shielding Jayme (novella)
Shielding Riley
Shielding Devyn
Shielding Ember
Shielding Sierra

SEAL of Protection: Legacy Series

Securing Caite (FREE!)
Securing Brenae (novella)
Securing Sidney
Securing Piper
Securing Zoey

Securing Avery
Securing Kalee
Securing Jane

<u>Delta Force Heroes Series</u>
Rescuing Rayne (FREE!)
Rescuing Aimee (novella)
Rescuing Emily
Rescuing Harley
Marrying Emily (novella)
Rescuing Kassie
Rescuing Bryn
Rescuing Casey
Rescuing Sadie (novella)
Rescuing Wendy
Rescuing Mary
Rescuing Macie (novella)
Rescuing Annie

<u>Badge of Honor: Texas Heroes Series</u>
Justice for Mackenzie (FREE!)
Justice for Mickie
Justice for Corrie
Justice for Laine (novella)
Shelter for Elizabeth
Justice for Boone
Shelter for Adeline
Shelter for Sophie

Justice for Erin
Justice for Milena
Shelter for Blythe
Justice for Hope
Shelter for Quinn
Shelter for Koren
Shelter for Penelope

SEAL of Protection Series
Protecting Caroline (FREE!)
Protecting Alabama
Protecting Fiona
Marrying Caroline (novella)
Protecting Summer
Protecting Cheyenne
Protecting Jessyka
Protecting Julie (novella)
Protecting Melody
Protecting the Future
Protecting Kiera (novella)
Protecting Alabama's Kids (novella)
Protecting Dakota

New York Times, USA Today and *Wall Street Journal* Bestselling Author Susan Stoker has a heart as big as the state of Tennessee where she lives, but this all American girl has also spent the last fourteen years living in Missouri, California, Colorado, Indiana, and

Texas. She's married to a retired Army man who now gets to follow *her* around the country.

www.stokeraces.com
www.AcesPress.com
susan@stokeraces.com

Made in the USA
Monee, IL
31 May 2025